D1246354

Joker's Wild

The Harry Starke Novels Book 18

Blair Howard

ISBN: 979-8-9862563-6-8

Dedication

For Jo my long-suffering but ever-patient wife.

Chapter One

Monday Evening 9pm

It was snowing. *Actually* snowing in Chattanooga, in December. It had come a couple of months too early and I knew it wouldn't last, and yet, it felt like something of a Christmas miracle.

I love living here in Tennessee because of the outdoors and the sunshine. Plenty of places to run, swim, golf and even fish, though fishing's not my bag. To be honest, I'd rather watch paint dry. No, except for the few short months of winter, the temperature's comfortable enough for T-shirts the year round. But snow in December? Now that was a big deal. Snow at Christmas? It hadn't happened in my lifetime, and I was pretty sure it wouldn't happen this time.

It was Monday, December 16, and I was at something of a loss. Construction on our office was finally complete, but it had been a royal pain in the... neck. And, with a full caseload and the holidays just around the corner, I hadn't been able to relax, nor had I been able to enjoy as much personal time as I would have liked to.

I was at home on Lookout Mountain. It was just after nine. Jade was tucked into bed while Amanda, Maria, and Rose had been busy most of the evening making tamales. Maria insisted tamales are a popular Latino food for Christmas parties. So that evening they did the prep work and planned to steam them in the morning.

I have to admit the kitchen smelled amazing, but it was also overflowing with plates, ingredients, and all three of their personalities as Maria taught them how to make the perfect tamale.

Me? I couldn't handle it. I had to get out of the house, which is why I found myself wandering the city that night, trying to clear my head. I would have gone to my father's house, but he was out of town, which is why Rose was with us. Now, you know I love female company, always have, but four? In one house? Come on! And so I was out on my own, walking the streets as I used to back in the good old days; something I hadn't done in many a long year.

It was inevitable then that I should end up on the Walnut Street Bridge on a night much the same as the one some five years ago when I watched a young woman throw herself to her death.

I'll never forget it. It was just after midnight. The wind was blowing. The ironwork singing. The snow blowing in off the river; small flakes flying fast, horizontal. I remember leaning over the parapet, staring down into the darkness... And I remember the lights from the aquarium and the Market Street Bridge sparkled on the surface of the water.

And, quite suddenly, there she was in the wind and snow, running, frightened, her heels clicking on the pavement, looking back over her shoulder as if she was being chased. I remember that she tripped and almost fell. I took a couple of steps toward her, but as soon as she saw me, she stopped, turned first one way then the other, looking desperately around, then she turned, ran to the rail, and...

I shouted for her to stop, then ran to her... But I was too late. She climbed over the rail and then she... jumped. She just... jumped. Bad... bad memories.

And there I was again: same bridge, same spot, same conditions—almost—cold, lonely, reliving the past... reliving a painful memory.

But that was five years ago. There had been many more such moments since then, and it was becoming more and more difficult to step away from the job. I couldn't forget Tabitha Willard any more than I could forget the rest of the victims—and villains—I'd dealt with over the years since I quit the police force back in '08.

So yes, my life has changed since then; drastically, some might say.

I was always wealthy, even when I was a cop, but now I'm a successful private investigator... an ex-cop with a brand new, classy office in downtown Chattanooga, a large client list—including the DA and just about every lawyer and judge in town, and even more in the big cities beyond: Atlanta, Nashville, Birmingham—and a family with a beautiful home on Lookout Mountain overlooking the city and the Tennessee River.

So there I was, back on the Walnut Street Bridge, trying to figure out exactly who and what I was, and remembering the past. Not just Tabitha, but Kate, Shady Tree, and my old friend Bob Ryan who was always there when I needed him, even when he wasn't. That doesn't make any sense, I know, not to you anyway. Now, after everything I'd seen, done, and experienced, I was still... I don't know how to explain it. Let's just say my head was a cauldron of boiling memories and I didn't know how to turn off the heat.

What I did know, and what you know, was that I was suffering from a dose of the holiday blues. Don't we all?

I gazed down into the water swirling around the bridge supports, shook my head, sighed and thought, *Well, I'm out. I might as well go and have a drink.*

I twirled my keys around on my finger, stepped away from the rail and walked the few yards back to my car.

After I slid into the driver's seat and pushed the starter button, the engine fired... and so did the radio: *Here Comes Santa Claus.* I snapped it off. There was no point in switching to a different station; not at that time of year.

I settled on the Sorbonne, another one of my old... actually, not so old haunts. It was a drive of less than a quarter mile.

I turned onto Prospect Street, intending to enter Benny's bar via the back door, to find the street jammed with police cars.

What the hell's going on? I wondered.

I managed to find a spot some fifty yards or so away on the side of the street and parked my car. I was about to exit the vehicle when my phone rang.

I looked at the screen. It was Captain Kate Gazzara of the Chattanooga PD, my one-time partner... in more ways than one.

"Hey, Harry," she said. "We have a situation at the Sorbonne. How soon can you get here?"

"Actually, I'm here," I said. "I just parked. What's going on?"

Kate didn't sound as surprised as I thought she'd be. "I think you'd better come on in," she replied.

I told her I'd be right there and ran across the street. Lucky timing, huh?

When I made it past the huddle of officers and entered

through the steel door, I found Kate just inside, waiting for me with a woeful look on her face.

"I'm so sorry. I... I'm glad you're here, Harry."

I frowned. "Sorry? Why are you sorry?"

"It's Benny... come on."

I went cold all over. I opened my mouth to speak, but the words wouldn't come.

She grabbed my arm and led me down the hall to his office.

"Benny?" I asked. "What... what happened? Is he all right?"

Kate didn't answer. And I knew. I knew, but my mind wouldn't accept it. Why else would a homicide captain be at the scene?

"Does he need us to look into something?" I asked, still in denial.

We entered his office, Kate first. It looked no different than it always did. A mess.

Benny wasn't at his desk.

"Kate, what the hell's going on? Tell me why I'm here."

"Did you know about his hidden room back there?" she asked.

"What? What room?"

She walked over to a file cabinet. It was usually set against the wall. It wasn't. It had been moved, turned away from the wall to reveal a narrow opening.

"I know nothing about that, Kate. I must have been in this office a hundred times..."

My mind was racing. *What the hell's Benny up to? Is he doing something illegal? What's in that room? Weapons? Drugs? Where the hell is he?*

"Come on," she said and grabbed my arm again, steering me toward the hole in the wall.

5

The room was small. Maybe twelve by twelve with a poker table set in the middle with seven chairs surrounding it.

The room was empty, the chairs vacant... except for one. Benny Hinkle was sitting at the table opposite the door, eyes wide, staring at us. And there were three gunshot wounds to his chest. My friend Benny was no more.

Chapter Two

Monday Evening 9:20pm

I couldn't stop staring. I wanted to look away, but I couldn't. My mind was telling me to, but my body refused to listen. I felt as if I'd been punched in the gut. Benny was my friend. *Who could have done this? To him?*

Benny was... different. He was a businessman, but unlike any I'd ever met. He was... short and way overweight, bald, almost always unshaven. He owned the Sorbonne. He was a nocturnal creature, aided in his endeavors by his trusty sidekick, barkeep and business partner, Laura Davies. They were a match made in hell, but somehow, they made it work.

I'd known Benny a long time, as long as I could remember, from my early days on the force. Back in the day, he was an antagonistic little creep, but over the years we grew to be friends. And, even in the early days, he was my number one CI, confidential informant. He was my go-to guy. If he didn't know it, he'd soon find out...

"Hawk and Robar are up front in the bar taking statements," Kate said, interrupting my thoughts. "I already talked to Laura. The poor woman's bawling her eyes out." Kate shook her head.

"She know anything?" I asked.

Kate shook her head and said, "No. No one saw anything. She said one of the customers had approached her... Apparently the guy had gone to the restroom. She said he came rushing back and told her he'd heard gunshots coming from back along the hallway. She said that at first she didn't take it seriously, but she did ask one of her staff members to go take a look. The girl came back, her face white and she was shaking. She couldn't speak... well, she just said 'Benny' and pointed back down the hallway. Laura said she dropped what she was doing, literally, she dropped a glass she was cleaning and ran down here and found the hidden door and peeked inside and saw him."

"Wow," I said. I felt numb.

Together, we looked over the scene. There wasn't much to see. A deck of cards, poker chips stacked neatly around the table. No money. No cigarette butts. Just Benny.

Clearly he was aware of and had been involved in a poker game and... the poor bastard had lost; big time. How long had it been going on? It was hard to tell, but it looked like a permanent setup to me. I stared at what was left of Benny for a long moment. It was difficult to see his body sitting there like that and not take it as some sort of message. *What the hell had you gotten yourself into?*

The room was like a prison cell: concrete walls, no windows. The only light in the room was the overhead above the center of the poker table.

"No weapon," I said thoughtfully.

"Yes, there is," Kate said. "It's on his desk. I don't know if it's the murder weapon, but I'm guessing it is."

I nodded and she followed me out into Benny's office. Sure enough, there among the clutter lay a government-issue Colt 1911 .45. Not one of those modern replicas. An original. It was old, probably made in the early 20s, and worth a tidy sum.

"Gloves?" I asked, holding out my hand.

She handed me a pair of purple latex gloves. I snapped them on, picked up a pen, slid it into the barrel, lifted the weapon to my nose, sniffed it, looked at Kate, nodded and carefully replaced it exactly as I'd found it, then stepped away from the desk.

"That's it," I said to Kate. "It's been fired, probably less than a couple of hours ago. I'm certain you'll get a ballistics match and, hopefully, some prints... If not, if the perp was wearing gloves, we have a premeditated murder on our hands."

"*Our* hands?" she asked pointedly.

I ignored her.

"If that gun belonged to Benny," I said, "someone must have known where to find it. Not only that, but they would also have had to have known about that room back there. That would be a small and select number of people: even I didn't know about it."

"Benny must have been part of the game—" Kate said before I interrupted her.

"He could have been," I said. "But it looks to me as if the game hadn't started, that Benny was setting it up... The shooter must have known about the secret space."

"Laura said she didn't even know about it," Kate replied, "and she's worked here... forever."

"I wonder who the players were," I said, scanning the

table. The deck of cards was at the center of the table and chips were set at six of the seven places, but none in front of Benny. *Hmm... Was he just the dealer, then?* I wondered.

"The seal on the deck hasn't been broken," I said and looked at my watch. It was just after nine-thirty. "Too early, I guess. I wonder who they are... the players," I said, more to myself than to Kate. "Anyone up front know?"

"No," she replied. "As far as we know, none of the staff knew about this room. Most of them didn't even know Benny played serious poker. He'd sometimes sit in on the games out in the bar, but this... No."

I shook my head, staring through the opening into the secret room. "You'd think somebody would have seen something," I said. "Six people... It makes no sense."

"Not necessarily," she replied. "Not if they came and went through the rear door on Prospect Street. I doubt you'll find anything on his security system, either. It's antiquated and rarely works."

I shook my head, turned, re-entered the room and took another look at the body. It looked pathetic. I leaned in close. I was going to close his eyes but thought better of it. Doc Sheddon was on his way and would pitch a fit if anyone touched the body before he did.

I stood back and looked again at what was left of the man I'd known for so many years, and I felt... I don't know... Sad? Yes, that, for sure. In life, there hadn't been much to like about him. He was an obnoxious little... He wasn't likable, but somehow he and I got along. I knew almost nothing about his personal life, though I figured he must have had a family somewhere, and that it was safe to assume they'd be devastated by his unfortunate demise. This would undoubtedly be their worst Christmas ever.

"Come on, come on, come on." I heard a voice out in the

hallway. "Out of my way. Let the mouse see the cheese." It was Doc Sheddon.

I stepped out of the room as he stepped out of the hallway into the office.

"Kate," he said. "And Harry. Why am I not surprised to see you here? He's in there, I suppose." He nodded at the opening. "Well, get out of the way. I don't have all night. Things to do. Things to do. Let's see what there is to see," he said and, without waiting for an answer, stepped forward, hoisted his big black bag over the edge of Benny's desk, and eased himself sideways through the opening into the visibly oppressive room.

I followed him in, then stood back and watched as he went to work. Kate stepped in and stood on the other side of the opening.

It didn't take him long. He checked Benny's neck—though why he did that, I've no idea because the man was obviously dead—shook his head, muttered something unintelligible, then took a thermometer from his bag and shoved it into Benny's liver.

He stood back, waited for a minute, then retrieved it, glanced at it, nodded, wiped it off, put it in a ziplock bag, sealed it and then returned it to his bag.

"There's nothing more I can do in here," he said. "Have them load him into the wagon as soon as the photographer's finished with him, will you, Kate?"

She nodded and opened her mouth to speak, but before she could, Doc said, "You want to know the time of death, I suppose? Between ninety minutes and two hours ago. Seven-thirty, give or take thirty minutes. The body's still warm. Liver temperature is ninety-six-point-one. Rigor has barely begun. Very few signs of lividity. Two hours max. Cause of death? Pretty obvious, don't

11

you think? I'll pinpoint it when I do the post tomorrow afternoon. Now, if you don't mind, I'm off to better things."

And with that, he closed his bag, grabbed it, eased himself back through the opening into Benny's office and then disappeared into the hallway shouting over his shoulder, "See you tomorrow, Kate. Merry Christmas, Harry."

"To unlock this room you need a key," Kate said thoughtfully as she fiddled with the knob of the door into the secret room. "It looks like it can be locked from both sides." Then she looked at me and said, "Harry, I know that look—"

"I want in on this, Kate," I said, interrupting her.

She closed her eyes, shook her head, then opened them again and said, "As if I didn't know."

She looked over my shoulder at Benny's mortal remains, frowned and clamped her lips together.

She locked eyes with me and said, "I'll need to get clearance from the chief."

"Clearance or not, I'm on it. Better with consent than without, though."

She nodded.

I picked up a poker chip from the table and turned it over in my fingers, stared at it. The little room smelled... stale. A lack of windows will do that. Funny thing was, though, it was a whole lot cleaner and tidier than Benny's office.

It was around that time that Mike Willis and his CS team arrived, but by then Kate and I were outside in the cold night air. The snow, sleet, whatever you want to call it, had quit, at least for the moment, for which I was thankful. I needed to get the stale smell of Benny's little chamber of horrors out of my system.

So, together we stood there, silently for a moment, then I asked her, "Where's your partner tonight?"

"Which one?" she replied smiling.

"Corbin. That's his name, right?"

She nodded. "Sergeant Russell has the night off. I figured you'd be here so I didn't bother to call him out."

"How about your other partner?" I asked. "The big hairy one?"

"You mean Samson? He's over there in my car." She pointed.

"Let's go say hello to him," I said.

Samson, a hundred-pound plus long-haired German shepherd, was a new addition to Kate's team. A rescue dog. Kate took him from a crime scene where he was guarding the body of his previous master. The two hit it off right away. He wasn't—still isn't—a canine officer, though he was made an honorary one after he saved Kate's life a few weeks ago. He made friends with just about everyone at the PD, including the chief. He is, however, something of an anomaly. He'd obviously been trained by an expert. Totally obedient but will attack in an instant if he thinks Kate's being threatened. I'd already met him a couple of times and a more lovable dog you couldn't find. Appearances, though, are deceptive. Especially so where Samson's concerned.

"Hello, fella," I said as we approached Kate's unmarked cruiser. The windows were cracked open a couple of inches and he was doing his best to greet me. His top lip was curled back showing his teeth. It was a look that would scare the frickin' pants off you if you didn't know better, which I did. I knew he was just smiling at me.

Kate slid into the driver's seat and rolled down the rear window so he could stick his head out, and... he and I, we had a quiet moment. There, is, something about the company of a good dog that will calm the soul, and I really did feel better after the moment.

The sleet was beginning again, so Kate rolled up the window to keep it out of the car and we returned to the rear entrance of the Sorbonne.

I may have mentioned it before, but I never really knew Benny, not in the truly personal sense. It was always a case of what you see is what you get, but I was learning more and more about Benny and his priorities, and I found it sad when I thought about how we never really find out about the real person until after they've died. All the secrets come floating to the top, like scum on a pond.

"Where's Laura?" I asked Kate. "Has she gone home?"

"No, she's still in the bar," she replied. "No one's gone home yet."

"I think we need to talk to her."

"Me too," she said. "Let's go."

Chapter Three

Monday Evening 9:50pm

The Sorbonne bar, a vast room some eighty feet long and half again as wide, with a long wooden bar that stretched most of the way along the south wall, was usually a dark and dismal place. From the name—The Sorbonne—you'd think it was an upscale watering hole, but it wasn't. I once heard it described as "a boil on Chattanooga's ass."

It was, in fact, one of the city's sleaziest bars, although Benny liked to call it a nightclub. It was the last refuge of every lowlife that could afford the price of a drink... But you know what? I liked it just the way it was. I'd begun patronizing the place when I first made detective back in '02. Not out of choice, not then anyway, but because it was a place where I could keep tabs on said lowlifes and gather a little information, mostly from Benny, who soon became my go-to guy, my CI, my confidential informant.

I'd known both Hawk—Sgt. Arthur Hawkins—and his

partner—Detective Ann Robar—for most of my professional life. They were sitting together in one of the booths.

I told them "Hi" in passing and headed for the east end of the bar where Laura was dabbing her eyes.

Laura Davies was Benny's business partner. At the time of Benny's murder I didn't know exactly how much of a partner she was, but later I found out she owned a big chunk of the business: thirty-five percent, in fact.

She's quite a character, is Laura. A modern Daisy Duke: long blonde hair she always wore in a ponytail, usually attired in a tank top that barely covered her breasts, cut-off jeans and cowboy boots. She rarely wore much makeup. She was the quintessential Southern barkeep, but it was all a facade. Laura is the happily married mother of two teenage kids. At work, she dresses for effect... and for the tips.

As soon as she saw me walk across the room that evening, she ran around the end of the bar to me, wrapped her arms around my neck and started crying again. I gave her a moment, trying not to let my own emotions get the better of me, then I pushed her gently away.

"Laura," I said, holding her by her shoulders, "I'm going to find who did this. That's a promise, okay?"

She nodded and wiped her eyes.

"Look," I said. "I know you've already answered a lot of questions tonight, but do you think you can walk me through it one more time? Anything you can remember will help end this quickly."

Laura looked up at me and said, "I'm so sorry, Harry. I don't have any answers for you. I really don't."

I nodded and gently wiped a smudge of mascara from her cheek with the back of my forefinger, then said, "Did you know about that secret room in Benny's office?"

"Well..." she began, "I told the cops I didn't. And really, I didn't know anything for sure. But, I had a feeling that there was something going on with him."

"I'm not here to judge him," I said. "I'm here to find his killer. Talk to me, Laura."

She exhaled and said, "I told you. I didn't know about that room. I didn't know he was a poker player... well, except that sometimes he'd sit in on a game out here in the bar, but that wasn't often. I swear. If anyone was playing poker with Benny back there, I never saw them. They would've had to have come and gone through the back door on Prospect Street.

"Sometimes he'd have friends back there in his office. You've been back there with him yourself, many times. A lot of people he knew would come to see him through that door, just like you, because it's more convenient. I didn't even know he was here tonight! He said he was taking the night off so he could take care of some things for Christmas."

That makes sense, I thought. *If he and his friends were in that hole in the wall, and the light was off in his office, you'd never know he was here.*

"So you hadn't seen him all day?"

Her eyes welled up as she shook her head.

"Did you talk to him at all? Text him. Phone calls?"

"No, Harry. No!"

I could see she was trying her best, but I could also see I was getting nowhere.

"When did you last see him?" I asked.

"Last night. I left early, around ten. That was the last time I saw him."

I nodded and said, "What kind of a mood was he in?"

"He was in a good mood... for him. He was always a little, you know, irritable. That's how he was."

"Was he worried about anything or... anyone?" I asked.

"No, not that I know of."

"Did he owe anyone money?"

"I don't think so, Harry, but then I wouldn't know anything about anything like that. He was very... closed-fisted when it came to his money."

"D'you know of anyone who might have had a grudge against him?"

"Ha. You know how he was better than anyone," she replied. "He managed to piss people off all the time, but no, I don't know of anyone who would have done something like this."

I still had my hands on her shoulders. I looked down into her eyes and said, "Okay, that's enough for now. Thank you, Laura. If..."

She took that half-step forward and wrapped her arms around my neck and hugged me. I hugged her, and we stood there for a long moment until finally, she whispered, "Thank you, Harry. I'm glad you're here... He didn't deserve this. You know he didn't."

"I know," I said as I gently pushed her away. "Whoever it was, I'm going to find him and... That's a promise."

Chapter Four

Monday Evening 10:30pm

It was just after ten-thirty when I left the Sorbonne that night. I told Hawk and Robar goodnight, and Kate walked me out to my car. Prospect Street was still choked with official vehicles; access at both ends was blocked by yellow tape guarded by uniformed cops.

"So," she said as we strolled to where my tricked-out Range Rover was parked. "What d'you think?"

"I think... I know it's going to be one tricky son of a bitch to solve," I said. "We have nothing other than the body, three slugs, three shell casings and an antique weapon that's almost certainly been wiped clean, and I'll bet my last dollar it belonged to Benny."

I looked sideways at her. She was strolling along with her head down and her hands clasped behind her back, and I shook my head and smiled to myself. *Same old Kate,* I thought, remembering the good old days when she was my partner, when she was a sergeant. She's come a long way since then, and I'm proud to think I might have made a small contribution to her success.

"Didn't you always tell me to stay positive?" she said. "That something will turn up, that it always does? Now look at you, Harry. You're on a huge downer... either that or you're getting old."

She looked at me and grinned.

"Old? Me? Come on. I'm only three years older than you."

"Yes, well, so maybe it's the easy family life then. Maybe you've gone soft."

"Screw you, Kate," I said, grinning at her.

Again, she looked sideways at me, gave me one of her inscrutable smiles, but said nothing.

By then we'd reached my car. I touched the button to unlock it. Then turned to face her.

"So," I said. "I'll see you tomorrow. You bringing the puppy and Batman and Robin?"

"Samson, Hawk and Robar? Yes, of course, if that's okay. Oh, and by the way, I texted the chief and told him we're collaborating. I got a one-word reply: 'Good!'"

"Geez," I said. "He doesn't change much, does he?"

"Not at all," she replied. "You drive home safe, you hear?"

And with that, she turned and walked quickly away, back to the Sorbonne.

On any other day, I would have climbed into my car and headed for Broad Street and from there to Scenic Highway and on up the mountain. But that night... The streets downtown were mostly quiet. It was the way of things. When the nights draw in—dark at five o'clock—the cold air sends most people back into their homes, or into the restaurants. But that night, instead of heading straight home, I sat for a moment in my car, thinking. I was... antsy, rattled, uneasy. I shook my head, trying to rid myself of that awful feeling that this one, this case, despite my promise to Laura, was going to get the better of me. It didn't work. I decided that it was too early to go to the house.

I'll take the long way home, I thought.

Actually, there is no long way home. Scenic Highway, Ochs Highway: they're about the same, just different. I took Ochs, and I drove slowly. And as I drove, I had time to think.

My first thought was of the irony of it all. I'd gone out that evening to clear my head and landed myself in yet another impossible case.

Benny Hinkle, was my second thought. *Shot dead. Why?*

I'd bickered with the man for years, even back in the day when I was a cop. He always had something wiseass to say, and he was always determined to have the last word, even if it didn't make any sense.

And now here I was, driving home late at night, in the rain and snow, in December and... would you believe, missing the poor guy.

Never, in a million years, would I have pegged him as someone who would die, murdered in such a... cold-hearted way. Benny liked to talk, sure. And yes, I'd seen him almost get in a fistfight or, more often than not, break them up when they broke out in his bar, which was often, I might add. But he wasn't a violent, angry man. If he was, I never saw it.

He'd been terrified of Don Tito and the mob when they'd shown up at his establishment looking for me. He certainly wasn't the kind of man who'd involve himself in a shootout. *I did like that 1911, though. Mike Hammer carried one just like it.*

21

It all just felt wrong. I couldn't think of anyone I'd ever met who would've gone after Benny. I figured his murder must have been either a spur-of-the-moment thing, or a misunderstanding gone way too far. If not, we were about to pull some major skeletons out of Benny's closet.

I turned off Ochs Highway onto Fleetwood, made a right onto Scenic, then a left onto East Brow. I was almost home. Most of my neighbors had decorated their homes with Christmas lights, mostly bright LEDs, but a few still had the old, classic chunky bulbs that radiated warm red, green, and yellow tones. They'd wrapped them around spandrels, porch beams, along the gutters and railings. We, Amanda and I, had put ours up together, and boy was it a pain! Running extension cords from the garage around the rest of the house, getting up on the ladder. I felt like Sparky Griswold in National Lampoon's *Christmas Vacation*. I even had an entire chain go out. But when all was said and done, it was worth it.

I parked my car in the garage and left my shoes by the back door. The lingering scent of tamale prep, mixed with a Christmas cookie candle in the living room, was... after what I'd just gone through, almost more than my stomach could stand.

I found Amanda in the living room curled up on the end of the couch. Rose next to her. Amanda was wearing little more than a huge, heavy-knit gray sweater, cradling a big mug of hot chocolate in her hands. The twinkling of the tree the perfect backdrop for her blonde hair. Her pale green eyes sparkled. She and Rose were talking together about some movie Rose was insisting we needed to watch. Jade was in bed. Maria was in the kitchen making more hot chocolate.

"Harry," Amanda said, swinging her legs off the couch.

"It's almost midnight. Where have you been? I was worried about you." It was then she saw the look on my face. "Oh my God, Harry. What's wrong?"

"I've just come from the Sorbonne," I replied. "Kate called me. Benny Hinkle's dead. Murdered... I need a drink. I'll be in the kitchen." And with that I turned and walked out of the room

I went to the kitchen, said good evening to Maria and asked her to give me a moment. She nodded and, without saying a word, left the room. I guess she could see what kind of a mood I was in.

I took a bottle of Laphroaig and a large glass from the cupboard, poured myself a more than generous measure, added a splash of water and took a sip. The fiery liquid burned my throat, but it felt good and seemed to calm my nerves a little.

I found a plate of sugar cookies on the countertop and helped myself to one, then stood at the window, glass in one hand, cookie in the other, staring out at the pool lights.

Two minutes later Amanda came in and joined me at the window, mug in hand. I looked down at it. The marshmallows bobbed. She slid her free hand around the back of my neck and squeezed my shoulder.

"Not feeling very Christmassy, huh?" she asked as she laid her head on my other shoulder.

"Benny's dead," I said.

"I know. I heard you."

She gave me a minute. She'd never been a huge fan of Benny Hinkle. She didn't care for his attitude, and some of the stories I'd told her in the past hadn't helped matters either.

"How... how're you feeling?" she asked.

"Kind of... numb," I replied. "He was shot three times in

the chest. He was just sitting there, at the card table... staring at me. It was..." I stopped, took a sip of whisky, then said, "I know you didn't like him... a lot of people didn't, but I can't... I didn't see anything like this coming."

"Well, you know how I felt about him," she said. "but this is horrible, Harry. I'm so sorry." She squeezed my shoulder again. Her hair smelled like coconut shampoo.

I was tongue-tied. I was having difficulty finding the right words. It was something I'd never experienced before. I was trying to tell her I wasn't going to let it go.

"We're so busy," I said. "Jacque's going to have a fit, but I can't just leave it to the department. Besides, I promised Laura... You know?"

"I do, Harry," she replied. "He was your friend. I understand. You must do what you have to."

I nodded, lost in thought, but sublimely conscious of her body next to mine.

She rose up on bare tiptoes, kissed my cheek and said, "I'm going to bed. Please don't be too long."

"No," I replied, still staring out of the window, "not too long."

And she left.

Me? I downed the rest of my drink, rinsed out the glass and set it on the draining board, then went to our bathroom and took a hot shower.

Ten minutes later I slipped into bed and Amanda rolled over, wrapped her arms around me and slid her right leg over me. She was... Never mind.

Chapter Five

Tuesday Morning 8:30am

My new offices were state of the art. Jarvis Jeffries, our interior designer, was almost done. In less than a month most of the rooms had been decorated and furnished. My own office was not quite as... I'm going to use the word "inviting" as my old office, but that doesn't really describe what I mean. I missed my fireplace, for one thing, and it was a little on the austere side but, on the whole, I was happy with it.

Jeffries and Amanda had worked together choosing my furniture. The desk was huge, sleek and modern, made from walnut. My chair was... not quite what you'd expect. It was one of those space-age things—black leather with red trim—designed to alleviate back problems; not that I had any, but Amanda insisted that prevention was better than a cure. Two comfortable armchairs for clients took pride of place in front of my desk. A large coffee table flanked by two dark leather sofas occupied the center of the east end of the room. The walls were painted magnolia. Six paintings by local artists were placed strategically around the room. Best of all, though, was the vast, glass north wall—floor to ceiling, end to end—that provided an unbelievably stunning view of the Tennessee River and beyond. Yes, I could live with that.

The lobby walls were painted a dark, ash gray and were hung with original paintings. The floor was cool brown and black. Two faded green leather couches and a half-dozen plants completed the first impression, as Jeffries called it. It was... impressive, and I was relieved that he hadn't overdone it. There was no clutter, no side tables, no magazines, just the paintings. I liked that.

The front office, directly behind the lobby, was, is, a utilitarian sea of six wood and steel desks.

Jacque's office, to the right of the front office, was only partially furnished at the time. She was still awaiting delivery of her desk and chairs.

The conference room, the brightest space—except for my office—in the building, painted in a color Jefferies dubbed seagull gray, was soon to become the nerve center of Starke Investigations. The walls, except for the giant monitor at the west end, were bare. The new table was a sea of dark oak; the chairs were comfortable and easily moved.

And there were eight small offices for the investigators, including a slightly larger one for TJ, who was our chief financial investigator.

At the far end of the central corridor, to the left, was Tim's... I'm not going to call it an office; it isn't. What it is is a dark world with a setup you might well see on the bridge of a starship. The walls were painted dark tan; Tim wanted black, but Jeffries absolutely refused and came to me in a hissy fit. So, we settled for dark tan. Tim's roll-around chair was at the center of a semi-circle of ten fifty-four-inch monitors, five over five. Don't even ask me what that setup cost. Every time I looked at it, I mentally thanked Jacque for making sure the old offices were well insured.

Yes, it was a stunning setup, and I was proud of it. That Tuesday morning, however, I was in no mood to appreciate it. I knew I was in for a fight with my staff, Jacque in particular.

I called a meeting for eight-forty-five. Everyone except the office staff was expected to attend, that included my business partner, Jacque, TJ, Tim, Heather and six other investigators. Kate was also there, along with her dog, Hawk and Ann Robar—I never quite knew what to call her, so I did as Kate did; I called her Robar.

By eight-forty-five they were all in their seats around the table, laptops, tablets and notepads at the ready; the three cops at the far end of the table facing me. Samson sat quietly on a short leash at Kate's side.

I was seated at the head of the table with my back to the monitor. I opened the meeting with a statement.

"Benny Hinkle was murdered last night. He was shot to death at the Sorbonne."

Tim dropped his pen, then shuffled in his seat and bent down to grab it. Other than that, the room was silent; I mean *silent!* They were all stunned.

I ran a hand through my hair, leaned on the table, looked around the assembly then said, "I know we're busy, but we're in this until we find the killer and put him away. We're collaborating with the police department... which is why Kate and her team are here. TJ, Heather, you'll be working with me. Tim, you'll serve as backup. The rest of you, I'll draw upon as I feel the need. Everyone understand?"

There was a rumble of voices around the room and I

could see that Jacque was itching to say something, but TJ beat her to it.

"Harry," he said. "I'm sorry to hear about Benny. But…"

I stared at him. He gave a quick laugh, shrugged, then continued, "We've got a lot on our plate right now. The agency is understaffed, and we already have more cases than we can handle."

I didn't answer. I wasn't able to because Jacque, sitting up in her seat, said, "I'm with TJ, Harry. I'm sorry to hear that Benny died, but we are already overwhelmed. There are a lot of people depending on us, including DA Larry Spruce. We're used to being busy, but now is not a good time to take on a major case, it being so close to the holidays."

I continued to stare at them. I don't know what kind of an expression I had on my face, but I'm pretty sure I didn't look happy.

"A man's been shot to death," I said slowly. "Someone we all knew. Someone who helped us many times in the past. Not only that, I promised Laura we'd find his killer."

Jacque closed her eyes and exhaled through her nose. "We don't have the resources right now, Harry. I know Benny was your friend, but I think the PD can handle it just fine."

"Yeah," TJ agreed.

I saw Kate looking at me from the end of the table. Her eyebrows were raised in question and the corners of her mouth were turned up in a tight smile. Hawk had his arms folded across his chest. Robar? I couldn't read her. Tim? He was visibly shaken. He couldn't look at me.

I saw TJ open his mouth to speak, but before he could I slapped the tabletop with the palm of my hand.

"Stop…! Stop," I said quietly. "I don't care how busy we

are! You don't think I know how busy we are? I know as well as y'all do."

I was angry. I could feel my face flushing. Why was I so angry? To this day I don't know. To be perfectly honest, I knew they were right, but I also knew I was right. And at that moment...

"Look," I said. "I'm just as tired as the rest of you. And I see the stack of cases on my desk. I see it every time I sit down, but I don't care. We can add one more to the pile. We've done it before. Solving Benny's murder is our top priority and it's not up for discussion."

Tim nervously fumbled with his glasses. Heather was looking down at the table. TJ and Jacque both had stiff expressions on their faces, but they were done talking.

"We need to move things around," I said. "Do whatever needs to be done to free us up. I want this done and finished by Christmas Eve." I rubbed my eyes. "We're in a good place. We have Kate and her team on board, and Benny's entire staff is willing to cooperate... Tim!"

He jumped when I said his name. He looked frazzled.

Easy, Harry, I thought. *He's just a kid.*

Actually, he wasn't. He was twenty-six then and looked sixteen. I took a deep breath and softened my voice.

"Work your magic, Tim. Check socials. It's unlikely someone would be posting on Facebook that they murdered Benny, but you never know. Look for word about secret poker games. Look for chatter, anything you can find that mentions or chats about Benny and the Sorbonne."

"TJ," I said as I looked at him. "Your job right now is to dig into Benny's financials, including the Sorbonne. Okay?"

He nodded but said nothing.

"Heather," I said. She looked up at me and gave me a small smile. "I want you on the streets. Check in with your

CIs, any confidential informant you've ever used. What's the street chatter saying? See what you can find out about the poker game. Who did Benny play poker with?"

"I'll get right on it," she said, then looked at Jacque.

"Don't worry about it," Jacque said in an exaggerated Jamaican accent. "I'll handle it. You just do as Harry tells you to."

Jacque wasn't a happy camper.

"Okay," I said. "That's about it for now. The rest of you get back to work. Jacque?" I looked at her and smiled. "We need to talk!"

She glared at me.

I looked down the table at Kate and said, "Give us a minute. I'll see you in the lobby."

I waited until the room had cleared, leaving only Jacque sitting next to me.

I looked at her and said, "I know, I know, and I'm sorry. I really do know how busy you are, we are, but this is important to me."

She pushed her chair back and stood up. "You're the boss."

Then she turned and walked out, leaving me sitting there feeling like an absolute shit.

Finally, I sighed, stood and went out to see Kate, who was waiting for me in the lobby, Samson at her side.

"That went well..." she said.

Chapter Six

Tuesday Morning 9:30am

I told Kate we'd talk later, then grabbed a fresh cup of coffee and went to my office. On the way I passed by Jacque's office. On a whim, I stuck my head inside and said, "Hey, you. Everything all right?"

"I'm not talkin' to you," she said without looking up at me.

I grinned and said, "What did you say?"

"I said... I'm..." Then she realized what she was doing, looked up at me, laughing, threw a rubber eraser at me and said, "Oh... you... Yes, I'm fine. Now get out of here and let me do some magic to make this mess work for you."

"That's my girl," I said. "You want some coffee? You can have this one and I'll go get another."

"No! But thank you, and crawlin' will not get you nowhere."

"When did it ever?" I said. "Okay, you know where I am if you need me."

That's what I like about Jacque. She's one of the few people I know who never holds a grudge.

I continued on to my office, opened the door, stepped inside, closed it behind me and was immediately aware of the almost overpowering smell of newness.

I stood for a moment wondering how long the newness would last, then shook my head, went to my desk, sat down in that awful ergonomic chair and took a sip of my now not-so-scalding hot coffee.

I couldn't sit still in my chair. I couldn't focus on... anything. I even found myself having to resist the urge to knock a pile of papers off my desk. And then I realized what the problem was, so I picked up the phone and called Jacque.

"What is it now?" she asked.

"It's this damn chair," I said. "Get me a real one and donate this monstrosity."

"Harry, that chair is good for your back and your posture. Amanda chose it for you."

"I don't care. I hate it. Damn it, Jacque, I can't think. Get me a nice, comfortable leather chair."

"You're the boss," she said caustically and hung up on me. *Damn! Now I'm going to have to smooth things over again.*

I looked at the door, half-hoping someone would knock. Of course, no one did. Everyone was avoiding me. I stood up, walked around the desk and went to the window and stared at the river. It was raining again. The sky was... overcast, dark. The river was a sea of tiny whitecaps and needle-like splashes from the rain. It was a nasty day, but the view was still somehow beautiful.

My neck felt hot as I paced back and forth along the expanse of the great window. I was in one of those black moods and I was trying to shake it. It was more than just that damn horrible chair; I was suffering the aftershock of Benny's death.

Who was Benny playing poker with? I wondered. *And why that frickin' secret room? Why get caught up in something like this in the first place?*

I just couldn't stand it. I was dealing with a Benny I didn't know. And Laura? As far as I knew she kept her nose clean. *But how could she not have known about that secret room? When did he have it built? Was it already there when he bought the place?* That was my guess. *Let's hope she wasn't lying to the cops...* I thought. *Damn it!*

I sighed, shook my head, stepped over to my desk, picked up my coffee cup and looked inside it. It was empty, and a good excuse to get out of my office, if only for a moment.

As I walked to the breakroom my thoughts turned again to Benny. I didn't think he was smart enough to pull something like that off!

Come on, Harry, I thought. *Don't be so critical of the guy. He doesn't deserve it.*

Sorting through the cupboards for something different, I found some pods of hazelnut coffee and a mug Amanda had bought for me to celebrate the end of the renovations. They weren't quite done yet; we still had the armories to complete.

And then I got to thinking about Amanda. I smiled when I thought about how excited she was about Christmas this year.

It was our second holiday with Jade. The first... she was too young to appreciate it. This year would be different, and there would be a lot of baby-related gifts from my family. We'd been in the house on Lookout Mountain for a little more than three years. The renovations to the old structure had been almost as extensive as those to my new offices, but we'd struggled through it.

She'd spent almost a week decorating the tree—trip after trip to this store or that, looking for... Hell, I don't know. Whatever it was she must have found it because the result was stunning. The nine-foot tree a winter wonderland of snow, realistic-looking birds and woodland animals. Even I was beginning to feel the festive spirit tugging at me as I saw how happy she was.

Yes, I was in a festive mood, but it was also beginning to stress me out. I'd gotten her a few things for Christmas, things I knew she wanted. But there was no surprise. I still hadn't found the "big gift." She'd told me she didn't want anything, that she was happy with what she had. Oh yeah, and if you believe that I have some swampland in... Well, you get the idea.

But she'd had a tough year, what with the bombing of my offices on Georgia and that little sojourn down Old Mexico way. She'd been through almost nine months of physical therapy, not to mention worrying about me. So, I wanted to give her something special.

I set the coffee machine and started the brew, then rummaged around in the fridge for creamer. Tim, bless his heart, had been shopping and picked up a half-dozen different flavors. Why he needed so many choices I didn't know, but I was a fan of the buttered pecan so that's what I put in my mug. It made for quite a mixture: hazelnut coffee with butter pecan creamer. I added the contents of a couple of packets of sweetener, stirred the concoction and made my way happily back to my office. It was just after ten o'clock.

Our offices were mostly quiet for the rest of the morning. I half-heartedly skimmed through several open files, researching locations and details on my brand new iMac while I polished off one, then a second mug of coffee. By lunchtime the five cups of coffee I had since six that morning had done their work, and to say I was frazzled would be a major understatement; sheesh, I could barely sit still.

I was also kind of miffed. No one, not Kate, TJ or Tim, had given me any updates on what their labors had produced. And, as one does in such situations, I began to seriously question why I'd become a private investigator in the first place. I'd left the force because I couldn't stand the bullshit, the internal politics... the frickin' paperwork, of which there was now a pile six inches high on my desk.

So, I was sitting there wondering who I could dump it all on and get away with it when my cell phone rang. It was Kate.

"Kate... Thank God."

"Hey, Harry," she said. "I take it things are a little less than blissful at the offices of Starke Investigations."

"You could say that," I said. "It seems nobody's talking to me. I hope you've got something for me."

"I have. We need you at the Sorbonne. We found a hidden safe in the wall of Benny's secret hidey-hole. How soon can you get here?"

I closed my eyes and breathed a sigh of relief.

"I'll be there in thirty minutes."

I hung up, stuffed my phone in my jacket pocket, grabbed my keys and coat and all but ran out of my office, almost colliding with Tim.

"Hey, Harry, sorry," he said, wiping a hand on his pants. "I just wanted to let you know that I've been looking through hundreds of social media accounts, but I haven't found anything yet."

"Well. Okay. That's okay, Tim. Keep looking. I have to go out."

He looked at his feet. He was fidgeting.

"Is there something else, Tim?"

He cleared his throat, looked up at me and said, "I just wanted to apologize for... earlier. I'm really sorry about Benny. It's so close to Christmas, an' all. I can't imagine how you and his people are feeling."

I sighed and clapped my hand on his shoulder.

"It's all right, Tim. There's nothing to apologize for. It was my fault. I'd just come from the Sorbonne and I was... Let's just say I wasn't in the best of moods. This is going to be a tough one, Tim, and you know how much I rely on you."

He nodded, smiled at me and said, "Yes, sir. I do, and I appreciate it."

"Good lad. Now get your ass back in that expensive cave of yours and go to work. Find me something I can use."

I looked in on Jacque and told her where I was going and didn't know if I'd be back before she left.

She said she'd probably be there, whatever time it might be. Then she asked me if I'd had anything to eat. I told her not since breakfast but I'd get something later.

"Make sure you do," she said. And I left.

I actually made it through three Christmas songs on the car radio before I'd had enough and turned it off.

The truth is, my mind was in a whirl. The case was no more than a few hours old and we were still fishing skeletons out of Benny's closet.

I'd seen no evidence of a safe anywhere in that room. Neither had anyone else until Mike Willis and his team had arrived and shooed us all out. As I drove, I thought about that safe and the secrets it might hold. *It's a fair guess,* I thought, *that it's hiding money or... Sheesh, no?* My hands tightened around the steering wheel and I shifted in my seat as I ruminated about what else it could have been hiding.

Needless to say, after remembering some of Benny's encounters with members of the Miami Mob, drugs came foremost into my mind.

Snow—sleet really—was falling again as I parked as close to the back entrance as I could. I ducked under the yellow tapes, checked in with the uniformed officer at the door, signed his sheet, and he pushed the door open for me to enter.

I stepped inside what once had been Benny's inner sanctum—pigsty would have been more accurate—to find Hawk and Robar riffling around in Benny's office again.

"Hey, Harry," Hawk said. "Welcome back to hell."

I was about to ask where Kate was when she marched into the room and said, "I don't know why I would have thought you'd come in through the front entrance. Don't even go there," she said as I opened my mouth to speak. "We got the safe open."

"And?"

"See for yourself," she replied.

The safe was set into the wall and covered with what looked like a steel vent cover. *No wonder we didn't notice it,* I thought. But it wasn't that that caught my eye; it was the stacks and stacks of cash on the poker table. Bills were wadded roughly together and secured with rubber bands. I picked up one of the stacks and riffled it; they were all hundred-dollar bills.

"This is a huge sum," I said, stunned. "All this was in the safe?"

"Yes, and—"

"How much is there, Kate?"

"Half a million."

She seemed to be resisting the urge to smile when I turned to look at her, my mouth gaping open.

"Half... a... million?" I mouthed, barely loud enough for her to hear. "Seriously?"

"Seriously. Trust me, we counted *several* times."

I stood there, incredulous. "Benny had half a million dollars in cash, just sitting in a safe in this... frickin' hole in the wall?"

"Quite the story, huh?" she replied.

"Was there anything else in the safe?"

"No. We've been trying to find a ledger or some sort of notebook, but so far... nothing, and I'm not hopeful. If he managed to keep this big of a secret from his business partner, I don't think Benny would've been careless enough to leave papers lying around in his desk drawers."

"Have you searched his apartment?" I asked, then immediately wished I hadn't. She gave me a look that could have killed a cat.

"What kind of a question is that?" she asked. "Of course we have."

"Well... Did you find anything?"

"Nothing."

"And Laura didn't know about this either?"

Kate pursed her lips and nodded, flashing her brows up and down. "She didn't. She's sticking to her story that she didn't even know about the room."

"D'you think all of this is from his poker games?" I asked.

Kate nodded slowly, but me? I was still too stunned by the enormity of the sum. *All from playing poker? I don't think so.* I couldn't keep from shaking my head.

"That's one hell of a stash to rack up playing poker with your buddies," I said.

"We haven't gotten any names or numbers yet," Kate said as she slipped her hand into her pocket and took out a business card. "Except for this one. It's Benny's lawyer. Bill Perks."

Chapter Seven

Tuesday Afternoon 12:30pm

Laura looked like a deer caught in the headlights when she joined us in Benny's office. Her eyes were the size of saucers.

"Harry," she said, agitated. "I told them. I didn't know about all this money." Her voice broke on the word "money," and she started sniffling. "I told you and the police I didn't even know about the room. You have to believe me, Harry. This is all too much. I have no idea what I'm going to do, but I'm telling the truth; I didn't know."

Hard as it was to trust people sometimes, I believed Laura.

"Okay," I said. "Okay. I believe you. Just... take a deep breath and listen to me."

She nodded, sniffed and seemed to calm down a little.

"Do you know this guy?" I asked, handing her the card Kate had given me. "He's Benny's lawyer.

She shrugged. "I know his name, but I've never spoken to him, never seen him in person or anything." She handed back the card, tucked a lock of hair behind her ear and rubbed her eye with the back of her hand.

I nodded, thanked her and told her that was all I needed for now. She hesitated for a moment, seemed about to speak, then turned and went back to the bar.

"Give me a minute, Kate," I said. "I'm going to call the lawyer."

She nodded, and I stepped out back onto Prospect Street and dialed the number. It wasn't raining, but the air was cold and I pulled my jacket collar tighter around my neck. *Let's hope this Bill Perks is willing to talk,* I thought as I listened to the phone ringing.

"Perks."

"Mr. Perks," I said. "Harry Starke here. If you've got a minute, I'd like to talk to you about your client—"

"If this is about Benny Hinkle's death," he snapped, interrupting me, "I already know all about it."

"I see," I replied. "So—"

"I'm checking something out," he said, his tone sharp and impatient. "I'll be at the police department later this afternoon."

"Look, Mr. Perks, if you could just—"

"I'm sorry, Mr... Starke, was it? I'm in the middle of something and I don't have the time to accommodate you right now. I told you; I'll be at the police department later this afternoon. Now I have to go." And with that he hung up.

Easy to talk to? Sheesh. That was weird.

I sighed, shoved my phone back into my pocket and went back to Benny's office. I was planning on giving Kate an update, but she was talking to Hawk, so I stood and waited, thinking about the call and looking idly around the secret room, when I noticed something. I don't know why it

41

caught my eye, but it did. At the top right corner of the doorframe, I spotted what looked like the head of a nail or screw. Again, I can't tell you why it grabbed my attention. Maybe something about it just didn't look right. I stepped up close to it and leaned in for a closer look.

"Mike," I said, turning to the CSI supervisor. "Have you seen this?"

He stepped up beside me and squinted, then he turned, grabbed one of the chairs and climbed up on it.

"Oh, yeah. I thought so. It's a camera."

"Tiny, huh?" I remarked.

Mike nodded, then felt with his fingers along the top of the frame.

"What d'you think?" I asked. "Is it a security camera?"

"No. I don't think so," he replied. "There are only two security cameras and we already pulled footage."

So, I thought, *we have a hidden camera. Who set it up? Benny? And if so, why?*

Mike climbed down and said, "I need to call in one of our techs before we go any further."

"Umm, you might want to hold off on that, Mike. I have a better idea. What do you think it's hooked up to? A monitor or something?"

"I don't think so," he replied. "There are no wires that I can see. I'm thinking it's a one-piece unit. I'm going to call in the techs."

"No," I said. "Not yet. Let me talk to Kate first."

Mike looked at me. He obviously wasn't happy that I was interfering, but he also knew I had the chief's blessing. So, he frowned, nodded and stepped out into Benny's office.

Me? I knew just the guy to handle it. I told Kate what we'd found and what I intended to do, then I made the call.

"Tim?" I said when he answered the phone.

"Hey, Harry. I'm still here at the office working on things. How's it going at your end?"

I told him first about Benny's safe and the funds he had stashed away and, as I expected, he asked me to repeat the amount.

"Oh, wow. I'll run this by TJ and see what he has to say. Cash is always tough to track down, though."

"Thanks, Tim," I said. "Do that, but that's not why I called you. I need you down here at the Sorbonne."

And then I told him what we'd found. When I finished filling him in, all I heard for a moment was... silence. Then I heard him moving around. Then, "Give me thirty minutes. I'm on my way." And he hung up.

Good, I thought. *Now maybe we'll get somewhere, I hope.*

The air in that back room and Benny's office was stale... No, it reeked. The damn place was like a tomb. Benny had never been the neatest person I'd ever met. There was always stale food lying around on top of file cabinets and the like, and that day was no different. I counted three empty pizza boxes.

I had to get out of there, and I did. I told Kate I was going to the nearby Subway to grab a sandwich and did she want anything. She told me no and I left. I swear, I must have been in and out of that back door a dozen times that morning.

I strapped in and fired up the motor.

Half a million bucks, I thought, *and Benny with three bullets in his chest.* The picture was starting to clear a little, but I didn't like what I was beginning to see.

Chapter Eight

Tuesday Morning Afternoon 1:25pm

I had just enough time to grab a six-inch turkey and swiss, eat it while I drove back to the Sorbonne, and wash it down with a tall container of tea before Tim arrived; he made it in twenty-five minutes. Mike and I led him to the secret room and showed him where the hidden camera was. Kate joined us a few seconds later.

Tim stared at the small black lens for a moment, then climbed up on the chair, slid his fingers along the top of the frame and, with a fingernail, he lifted a short section of the top of the frame, set it to one side then gently extracted the camera: a slim black box maybe two inches square and three-eighths of an inch deep.

"Nice one," he muttered to himself as he climbed down. "A spy camera."

"So, that's it?" I asked. "Where's the power source?"

"It's internal," he replied. "A battery... with a pretty long life. It's fully self-contained. It has a sixteen-gigabyte micro SD storage card. See?" Tim said and pushed a tiny protuberance on one side of the camera. A tiny sliver of black plastic with gold terminals popped halfway out. He pushed it back in and said, "Don't want to lose the little bugger. This is an expensive piece of equipment... and whoever installed it knew what he was doing." He turned it over in his fingers, stared at it for a moment, then continued, "The footage can also be automatically uploaded to a cloud so long as there's a Wi-Fi connection. Neat! Let's see what we've got."

He picked up his computer bag and went out into the office. Mike, Kate and I trooped out after him. He sat down at Benny's desk, opened his bag, took out his laptop, set it on the desk and opened it. Then he reached into one of the pockets on the bag and retrieved what I knew to be a card reader and inserted it into one of the USB ports. That done, he extracted the tiny card from the camera, inserted it into the reader and began clicking away; Kate, Mike, and I hovering over his shoulder.

"Okay, guys," he said, shrugging his shoulders as if to push us away. "You're going to have to give me a little space."

We obliged and he continued tapping, never taking his eyes off the screen. Then, after opening several files, he sat back in his chair and shook his head.

"Sorry, guys," he said, folding his arms and then pushing his glasses further up the bridge of his nose. "This is going to take a while... and with y'all looking over my shoulder I'm really nervous. I need to take it back to my office where I have the right equipment."

"Right equipment? Why? What's wrong with your laptop?" I asked.

"Nothing. It would just be easier and faster using my Enright... Look, this drive has been encrypted, and by someone with some serious tech skills. They've erected a kind of digital fence. That by itself will take some time for me to get through. But, there's also a fail-safe."

"Okay," I said slowly. "So..."

"This camera is connected to the Wi-Fi here, in this building. The data is, was automatically being uploaded to a particular cloud that I know I won't be able to access. In case there was a problem with that, this drive is like the backup storage. But, it's synced with the IP address for this building alone. If I use a different IP address, like the Wi-Fi at the office, all the data on here will be erased."

"So, the footage would be lost," Kate said, rubbing her temple.

Tim pushed his glasses up on his nose again. "Maybe... I might be able to do something with my IP scrambler. That way, we may be able to, uh, trick the camera into thinking it's still here."

Mike smiled at his choice of words.

Tim continued.

"It'd be a lot easier to work in my office than here on my laptop." He shrugged, looked up at me and said, "But, we still run the risk of losing the footage."

Kate held up her hand and said, "No way. You can't screw it up. No. I... whatever it was you said. The chief will never go for that. If you're going to do it, you'll have to do it here. I'm sorry it's not ideal, but I don't think I have to spell it out for everyone why the footage on this camera is so critical to the investigation."

Tim raised a hand and said, "No worries. I'll just take my time."

"And, whatever you find," Kate said, "we'll need copies of it." She looked sideways at me and said, "Harry?"

I nodded. "Of course."

"Anything we can get you, kid?" Mike asked.

Tim leaned forward and began typing furiously. "Yeah, please shut the door on your way out... Oh, and I'd love some coffee, please."

"I'll take care of it," I said. "I'll get you a sandwich, too. Be careful, Tim. I know you can do this."

I stepped out into the hall with Mike and Kate, closed the door behind me and sighed.

"You think he can do it?" Kate asked.

"If anyone can, it's him," I replied.

"I guess the big question for now is," Kate said, "do we think Benny set up the camera? Or, was it someone else?"

"I don't know why someone else would set up a camera if they intended to commit a crime. But if Benny set it up, he must have had help. He doesn't... didn't have the skills. I don't think it's a security camera, not in the literal sense of the word. I think he was using it to spy on the players, which means he was up to something really fishy."

"I think you're right," Kate said, nodding. "I mean, look at the rest of the electronics in this place. He doesn't even have a computer in his office, and his security system dates back to the stone age."

I nodded. "Good point. We'll give Tim some time and hope he can deliver the goods."

An alert chimed on my phone. "Shit! I have to go, Kate. I had an appointment with our security contractor to talk about the armory we are having installed. It's a good thing I put it on my calendar, or I'd have forgotten about it."

"Will you be back?" she asked.

"Yes, as soon as I can. Would you mind getting Tim some coffee and something to eat?"

She said she would, and I thanked her and went to my car.

What Tim had told us about the hidden camera got me thinking as I drove back to the office. It had all those security measures in place so people like me couldn't go poking around. Benny didn't know enough about computers and technology to do something like that himself. But he had a hidden safe in that back room with half a million dollars in it. If he didn't have the skills he needed, he sure as hell had enough cash on hand to hire the best in the business to do it for him.

I'd been looking forward to my meeting with our contractor, but at that moment it was all I could do not to cancel the appointment. I was knee-deep in the case and needed to stay on top of it, but I didn't... cancel. That would have been more than my life was worth. Jacque would have pitched a fit.

So, as I drove into the parking lot, I was hoping it would be over quickly so I could get back out on the streets and find out what really happened to Benny.

And why...

Chapter Nine

Tuesday Afternoon 1:30pm

John Oper, my safe-room designer, was all smiles and shook my hand firmly when I met him in the lobby that afternoon. He'd been chatting with Jacque and was holding a thick folder full of plans and photos of everything he wanted to cover. Just a quick glance told me that my goal of a short meeting and then out of there was in jeopardy. I wanted, needed, to be back at the Sorbonne when Tim cracked that memory card.

"Afternoon, Harry," John said and grinned. "Happy holidays to you."

"Thank you, and the same to you. I hope you haven't been waiting long."

"No, not at all. Jacque here told me how busy you've all been."

After a few more pleasantries, he dug into the meat of his presentation. I couldn't help but notice how his mustache bounced with every word.

"Your main armory here on the ground floor is going to

be state-of-the-art," he began. "I spent a lot of time researching the safety measures, as well as any other concerns you may have, and I've found the perfect layout for you." He flipped through a couple of photos.

I didn't blink.

"It'll be locked down like a safe room, as will the smaller armory upstairs. I think these gun racks are going to be your best bet. They're more sophisticated, in my opinion. Easy to access and customizable if you want to change the layout later on. We'll also install this bank of secure drawers."

"And these will all require codes or fingerprints to open?" Jacque asked.

"Yes. Installing this tech isn't as expensive as people first assume. You've got biometrics for everyone's phones now. We can easily get you and the employees set up with the system."

He cycled through several more drafts, with Jacque asking a majority of the questions; I just sat there and mostly listened. Once he'd finished his spiel, he stopped talking and looked at me, waiting for me to say something.

My mind was swimming. I wasn't quite sure what to say. I'd been listening the whole time as best I could, but none of what Oper said had sunk in.

"So," I began, clearing my throat. "You've worked with police departments all over the country, correct?"

He smiled proudly. "Yes, sir. Government facilities, too. I can promise you that both rooms will be safe."

I shrugged, looked at my watch and said, "Well, okay then. If you say so. Jacque, I'll leave the details to you."

Jacque nodded, looked at Oper and said, "John. Is there anything else we need to go over today?"

He looked from me to her, then sheepishly shook his head.

"No, ma'am. I gave you the dates of when we'll be in to start working, so I guess I'll see you both then."

Jacque thanked him for everything and saw him out. Me? I stayed where I was in the conference room, waiting for her to return, knowing I was in for an earful. She returned a few moments later, her eyes burning.

"Okay. You want to tell me what that was all about?"

You know, there are very few people in this world that can intimidate me; Jacque's one of them. Don't get me wrong. I love her to death, and I'm sure she loves me too. We've been through hell together, but she stuck with me through thick and thin. I don't know what I'd do without her.

"I've got a lot on my mind right now, Jacque," I said by way of explanation.

"You've always got a lot on your mind, Harry! You're a private investigator."

"Jacque, something new has—"

"Two weeks ago you couldn't wait to meet with John," she snapped. "Now when he's here in our office, you're practically chasing him out the door, rushing him and acting like you don't care. You barely listened to him."

"I know, and I didn't mean to handle the meeting like that, but it's routine stuff. You know the final decision is yours. Why you had to drag me into it in the first... Look, I'm sorry, okay? This Benny thing is front and foremost in my head right now and will be until it's solved."

"Harry." Jacque groaned, rolling her eyes. "Listen to me. We're all genuinely sorry about Benny. And, I'm sorry that we weren't as gung ho about working on his case as you'd like us to be. But we are all stressed, tired, and worn out, and it's only getting crazier with the holidays coming up, and now you've commandeered Tim. What am I supposed to do without him?"

She had a point. Tim handles our computer systems, all things to do with the internet, including operating and maintaining the company website. He also handles background checks and skip searches, and God only knows what else.

"I'm sorry, Jacque," I replied. "I'll get him back to you ASAP. In the meantime—"

"In the meantime," she said, interrupting me, "I suggest you go to your office and take a few minutes. You look terrible, like you haven't slept in a week."

"Geez," I said, shaking my head. "That was... cruel."

"Harry," she replied softly. "It wasn't meant to be. You're trying to do too much. I'm concerned about you, about your health. Look at you. Your eyes are all bloodshot. Please, try to slow down."

She looked at me. I nodded. "I'll..." I didn't finish it. I try not to make promises I can't keep.

She sighed and shook her head. "Okay," she said, rising to her feet. "Let me know when you leave... By the way, what have you bought Amanda for Christmas? You haven't forgotten, I hope."

"No, I haven't forgotten and, as yet, I haven't found anything."

"You want me to look for something for you?"

"Maybe. Leave it with me for a day or two, okay?"

"You only have a day or two," she said as she closed the door behind her.

I stared at the door wondering how the hell I was going to get through the next few days without making things even worse for her. I had no answers. All I knew was that I had to find Benny's killer. I got up from the table and went to my office.

It was four o'clock. A little too early for a drink, but what the hell. I went to the cabinet and took out a bottle of scotch.

I grabbed a glass, went to the breakroom for some ice, then poured a small measure over it. Not much; I was driving.

Swirling the whisky around in my glass, listening to the ice tinkling, helped me think. Was it too soon to head back over to the Sorbonne? Probably. I hadn't heard from Tim, and I knew he would've called if he'd found something. I looked at my watch again: four-fifteen.

"Hmm!"

I swiveled my fancy chair. My glass made a satisfying *ting*. I placed it on my desk in front of me, leaned back as far as the chair would go and closed my eyes. I needed answers. I needed to talk to Bill Perks. I needed the footage on the hidden camera to be revealing. I needed TJ to find a link between Benny's finances and the money in his safe. I needed to find who the poker players were and track them down. Most of all, I needed to find Benny's killer. On top of all that, I needed to find a Christmas gift for Amanda.

You're right; I needed one hell of a lot, and I was getting nowhere.

Chapter Ten

Tuesday Afternoon 4:45pm

our-forty-five, I thought as I was acquainting myself with the specks on the ceiling. *Geez, come on, Tim.* I had my feet up on the desk, my chair back as far as it would go, my hands linked together behind my neck. It wasn't the most comfortable position, due mainly to my brand new, back-friendly chair, but there I was, lost in thought staring up at the ceiling, and then my cell phone rang.

I dropped my feet to the floor, my chair sprang back, almost flipping me out of it, and I grabbed my phone from the desktop and glanced at the screen; it was Kate.

"Hey Kate, what's the good news?" I said, grateful for a break in the boredom.

"It's... huge, and I'm not sure it's good," she said. "You're not going to believe this. That lawyer you spoke to, Perks, he's here at the department and he has a woman with him. Harry, he says she's Benny's daughter."

My mind went blank, I mean literally. I could not believe what I was hearing.

"What? What did you say?" I asked after a long pause.

"Bill Perks is here and he has Benny's daughter with him."

"Benny has a daughter?"

"Apparently," she replied. "It's what she's claiming. We're looking into it, of course, but she's insisting that she has to talk to the police and you, Harry."

"I'm on my way. Don't talk to them until I get there," I said, leaping out of my chair. "I'll be there in twenty."

That was a bit optimistic seeing as how it was the middle of rush hour.

I had my coat on and my keys in hand when there was a knock at my door.

"Come on in," I yelled as I took one last look around to make sure I hadn't forgotten anything.

The door opened and Tim stepped in, tablet in one hand and his laptop case on his shoulder.

"Harry," he said, grinning. "Hey, I just got back. So, I managed to download the content onto my computer, and I think I've figured out a way to get around the IP issues so nothing will be erased."

I felt as if I was caught between the hammer and the anvil. I wanted to get out of there, but I also wanted to know what Tim had found.

"O...kay," I replied hesitantly.

"Yeah, see, I figured out a way to crack it but, like I said, it's heavily encrypted. It'll probably take me a while."

"But you're sure you can do it without screwing it up?"

Tim pursed his lips and nodded. "Yes."

"Good. I've got to go. They need me at the PD. Stay on it, but for God's sake, don't lose the data."

"You got it, boss," he said as he stepped out of the way.

I slapped him on the shoulder and rushed past him, stuck my head in Jacque's office and told her where I was going and then, without waiting for an answer, I rushed out to my car.

All these frickin' years and I didn't know.

I didn't even know if Benny had a family. Never once did he mention a daughter.

I steadied my hands on the steering wheel as I rolled out. The only sound was the slight scrape of my windshield wipers. It was snowing again, and it was heavy.

If she's who she says she is... Whew!

The police department was surprisingly quiet and, well known there as I am, I was able to sign in and head straight on up to Kate's office.

"I've got them in the family interview room," she said. "All of them."

"All of them?" I asked. "How the hell many are there?"

She just smiled and said, "Let's go see." And, together, we headed that way.

Laura was standing by the window, her arms folded over her chest, staring out over the parking lot: not one of the best views in Chattanooga.

Bill Perks and the "daughter" were seated together on a couch set against the far left wall.

I looked her over. If she really was Benny's daughter, I didn't see it. I figured she was in her mid-thirties. She had shoulder-length, curly blonde hair and hazel eyes. Her nose was long and slim, and she had a willowy frame. *Not bad looking. Maybe she takes after her mother.*

She was wearing skinny jeans with a cream top and a long red cardigan that hung over her body all the way down to her knees. Her feet were turned toward each other, the tips of her ballet flats touching.

She was leaning forward, forearms resting on her knees. She'd been crying. Her eyes were red, her cheeks flushed and she was clutching a clump of tissues in both hands.

"This is Harry Starke," Kate said to Perks. "You spoke on the phone, I believe."

He stood up and thrust out his hand. I heard Laura click her tongue.

Looking at him for the first time was... quite something. Never mind the daughter, Bill Perks could have been Benny's twin! He had the same stout, rough and heavy demeanor. Unlike Benny, though, Bill had a permanent scowl on his face—that because of the wrinkles around his mouth, eyes and forehead. Overweight, ugly and as well dressed as a lawyer should be for his day-to-day quest for his pound of flesh.

"We did," he croaked. He cleared his throat and looked down at his hand, waiting for me to take it, which I reluctantly did. His grip was exactly what I'd expected, sweaty and limp.

Geez.

"When you said you were checking something out," I said, "I'm assuming this is what you meant?" I nodded to the young woman still sitting on the couch behind him: same position except that she was looking up at me.

She got up and gingerly shook my hand.

"I'm... Trish Hinkle." She swallowed, then continued, "I'm sorry. I don't know what to do. I've never been in a situation like this before."

"I would have been very surprised if you had," I said, smiling sympathetically at her. "I'm sorry for your loss. Benny was a... friend."

Her eyes were awash. *Best to take it slow, Harry.*

"Benny was your father?" I asked.

She responded with a slow nod, her eyes darting to the floor. But that didn't necessarily mean she was lying, not in that situation.

Still looking at the floor, she fidgeted with her hair, tucking some of it behind her ear. She shrugged and slapped her hands on her thighs before reaching into her pocket. Clearly, she wasn't sure what else to do.

"My dad gave me this," she said, presenting me with a USB thumb drive, which I gently took from her.

Laura clicked her tongue again and, still gazing out the window, said, "Well, I've worked with your father for almost *fifteen years*, and he never mentioned you. Not once."

Oh boy. Trish shot her a weak glare. I could tell she was fighting to hold back the tears.

"Harry, Kate," Laura said. "I don't know what's going on here, but I don't believe a word of it. And I don't even know you," she spat as she turned and pointed at Perks.

"Take it easy, Laura," Kate said. Then she looked to the daughter and continued, "You said you wanted to talk to the police and Harry, Trish. What's on that flash drive?"

"My dad told me that if anything bad happened to him, I was to give it to Harry..."

She paused for a second. I looked at the drive in my hand, bit my lower lip, then looked at her. My mind had gone blank. *What the hell am I holding?* was all I could think.

Trish wiped a tear from her eye, sucked in a deep breath, shuddered and said, "I helped him record it a while back. He wanted the police to see it, and he wanted Harry to be there when you all watched it."

Perks rubbed his nose before snagging a tissue from a box on the coffee table. He didn't look sad. He looked... smug. His beady eyes flitted from Kate to me, then back to Kate again.

"I'm here on Benny's behalf, and now Miss Hinkle's. I suggest you watch the video. Then we'll discuss it."

Kate nodded. "I have a computer in my office. We can use that. If you'll follow me, please."

As we walked across the situation room, I could hear Laura asking questions, prodding Trish, asking her where she was from, how old she was, and why she'd never seen her at the Sorbonne.

"That's enough, Laura," Kate snapped. "Give her a break. She's just lost her father."

Laura answered with another click of her tongue, but she did as she was asked and said nothing more, not then anyway. Kate's promotion to captain had come with a much larger office, complete with whiteboards and a small round conference table.

Samson was lying on his bed under the window when we entered. He immediately got up and showed his teeth, smiling.

"Down, Samson," Kate said quietly, and the dog lay down again, front legs stretched forward, his chin flat on the floor between them.

"He won't bite, will he?" Trish said, cowering behind Perks.

"No. He won't bite," Kate replied. "Please, sit down." She waved a hand in the direction of the table. And we did.

Trish and Perks sat at the table together.

Me? I handed Kate the thumb drive and went to the window and stood next to Samson, my back to the windowsill, and folded my arms. The dog raised his head and looked up at me. I winked at him. He snapped his jaws, then lowered his head again to the floor.

"If you'll give me a minute," Kate said, "there are a couple of other officers I'd like to see this."

She picked up the desk phone, punched in a number, then said, "I need you, Hawk, Robar and Mike Willis in my office, now, please."

Just a few seconds later there was a knock on the door and Sergeant Corbin Russell, followed by the two detectives and the CSI supervisor, stepped inside.

"Take a seat, please, guys," Kate said. "I want you to watch something."

Then she sat down at her desk chair, plugged in the thumb drive and turned the monitor so we could all see it.

"Before you begin," Perks said, "I'd like to remind you all that the footage you're about to see may be Benny Hinkle's last will and testament."

Kate glanced at Bill Perks. He didn't acknowledge her, merely stared at the computer screen, waiting for her to start the video.

"Everyone ready?" she asked.

Everyone was.

She hit play.

Chapter Eleven

Tuesday Afternoon 5pm

The monitor screen flickered a couple of times and then we were gifted with a closeup of Benny's face squinting into the camera, then he backed away and sat down.

He was in a small living room. He sat down on what appeared to be a dining room chair set against a backdrop of a wood, paneled wall, his hands cupped together in his lap. He leaned forward, squinting at the camera, his brow furrowed.

"You sure it's recording?" he asked.

"Yeah, Dad," Trish said from behind the camera.

"I don't see a light or anything."

"Dad, it's my phone. It doesn't have a light for that, but I promise, it's rolling."

The conversation to that point almost made me smile. Typical parent, child bickering; typical Benny. That said, it was easy to see that he was stressed: the tone of his voice, his eyes, the way he blinked, sometimes rapidly.

"Hello. Uh... hello," he began. "If you're watching this, I'm dead!"

The opening statement was followed by a long pause.

Trish put a hand over her mouth and began to cry. She half turned away from me so I was unable to study her, to judge if she was faking or not.

Benny blew out a breath through his lips. It made a noise like a horse, then he continued.

"All I can say is, I hope I went quickly. I can't stand pain, as you well know, Harry... I have a written will talking about all of this, but I wanted to make sure I said it again, here, what I'm giving away." He smiled. A small, goofy smile. "I wanna make sure that whatever I have, my viper of a lawyer doesn't get his hands on it."

"Oh, Benny," Perks scoffed.

Laura looked at him and smirked.

"My daughter, Trish... Patricia, is to inherit all of my part in the Sorbonne. I own sixty-five percent. She is also the beneficiary of my life insurance policy. The face value is half a million. She is also to inherit ninety percent of my cash on hand and in my personal bank accounts. The rest of it, ten percent, goes to my partner, Laura." Then he listed several more items, including his home, his car, and other valuable possessions, all of them going to Trish.

"To my friends and loved ones, I want to thank you for putting up with me all this time. And, I really just want to thank you for being around when I needed you, especially you, Harry. You saved my ass more than once."

He thanked several more people by name—some I knew, some I didn't—including Laura. I glanced at her. The smirk was gone.

Then, he leaned back in his chair, placed his hands on his knees, and said:

"My last message is to you, Harry." He stared into the camera, folded his arms, took a deep breath, swallowed hard, and said, "Harry, you and me, we haven't always gotten along, but I've always thought of you as my friend, and I trust you. If somebody's offed me, then this is my last wish: I'm hiring you from the grave. I want you to find the bastard who killed me and break both of his arms... or hers. Trish will pay you whatever it takes, right, Trish?"

"Yes. I will," Trish said, somewhere off camera.

I looked at her. She looked at me. Tears were streaming down her cheeks, but she managed to nod her confirmation.

"That's it," Benny said. "That's all I got. Harry, you look after my kid for me, you hear? Goodbye, everybody." The screen went black.

Trish sniffled, wiped her face and looked at me, her eyes pleading. I nodded at her.

Before anyone had a chance to speak, Perks grunted and reached into his inner jacket pocket and took out an envelope, reached out and handed it to me.

"This is for you, Mr. Starke." Then he leaned back in his seat and stared at the black screen. It was as if he'd washed his hands of the situation.

"And, this is?" I asked as I opened the envelope.

"It's your payment. Or rather the down payment, for the job."

That it was. Ten-thousand dollars!

Kate stood up and said, "Harry, I need a minute. You, too, Mike. We can talk out in the hall."

Once the door was closed behind us, she shook her head and said, "Well, what do you think, Harry? Benny didn't look as if he was being forced to make that video."

I shook my head and said, "No, he wasn't being pressured, and that was Trish's voice in the background. He was... Anxious, nervous, but he wasn't under duress. It's hard to say for certain, but I don't think there was anyone else in the room besides Trish. And, from the way he was talking, she really is his daughter. We can't take anything off the table yet, but... He made that video because he had a hunch something bad was going to happen to him. A strong enough hunch for him to prepare for it. That's not something anyone does lightly, or without cause. He was into something big, and we need to find out what it was."

Mike nodded and said, "I agree. He made that video of his own free will... Your guy, Tim; he's still working on the hidden camera?"

"Yes."

"It would be my guess, then, that Benny had someone set that up for him," he said.

We kicked that theory around a little more. It was obvious he'd gotten help, but from whom? That was the question. Trish? On first impression she didn't strike me as the candidate. Did she have the skills to do it? As yet, we didn't know. Me? I hadn't said more than a couple of words to the girl.

"Did you talk to her at all?" I asked Kate.

"Not much. She didn't want to talk, not until you were present. She insists she's Benny's daughter and, after seeing that footage, I'm inclined to believe her. She's been living in Atlanta. She did say she didn't know her father all that well. No surprise, the shyster lawyer wouldn't let us ask any more questions until we saw what was on the flash drive."

"Can I talk to her now?"

"Sure, I think we need to move her to an interview room, though. Who else do you want present?"

"For now, just her. PI to client. Make sure Laura and

Perks stay. We might need to talk to them too, but not until I've talked to the girl."

Chapter Twelve

Tuesday Afternoon 5:35pm

I took Trish Hinkle back to the family conference room and settled her down on the couch with a fresh box of tissues, then I turned a chair from the table and sat down in front of her.

"Now," I said gently. "Are you okay?"

She nodded, then sniffed.

"Good. Now let's see if you and I can figure this out, shall we?"

Again, she nodded, looked at me, and then gave me a tiny shrug.

"So Trish, where have you been all these years?"

She bit her lip, then said, "I was living in Atlanta with my mom. She died three years ago from ovarian cancer."

"I'm so sorry, Trish. That must have been hard for you. So tell me about you and your father."

"I... didn't know him well," she replied. "I always knew about him, but it wasn't until after Mom found out she was sick that I met him. After that I saw him a few times, then at the funeral, then five or six times since. He used to give me some money."

"So you and he made the video... Did he ever tell you why?"

She shook her head, then said, "I asked him, but he just said he ran a club in Chattanooga and had to deal with some shitty people sometimes and that there was always the chance of him being killed in a robbery."

That made sense. "Did he ever mention anyone in particular that might want to harm him?"

She shook her head.

"Did you ever come to Chattanooga to visit him?" I asked.

"No... It wasn't that I didn't want to. He always told me it wasn't the right time."

"So, you saw him maybe... what, ten times in five, six years?"

"Umm... maybe a couple more times than that. He did come to see Mom once, when she was sick."

"Were they married?"

"Divorced."

"How old are you, Trish?"

"I'm twenty-seven. I'll be twenty-eight in March."

"How well did you get along with your dad?"

"I got along great with him. He was good to me... and Mom. He never missed a single child support payment... Mom said. And he always sent me birthday and Christmas cards with money in them. I kept them all. You can see them if you like."

The girl was talking about a Benny I didn't know.

"Look," she said. "I know we made that video, but I

didn't think something like this would actually happen. It still didn't seem real that my dad even asked me to help him record something like that."

I nodded and said, "I can understand that. You do realize what a shock it's been for all of us... you turning up out of the blue, like this? Nobody here even knew you existed."

That was a bit of an understatement. Laura was still in the building. After the video had wrapped, she'd confronted Trish. She couldn't believe that Benny had a daughter. She was also furious that Trish was the main beneficiary in his will.

"I knew coming here was going to ruffle some feathers. But I had to." She shifted on the couch. "My dad and I did keep in touch; not that often, but we did. He wasn't in my life the way my mom wanted him to be, but he always made sure we were okay."

"Why do you think he came back into your life?" I asked.

"Well," she began. "I don't know. When my mom died, Dad started checking in with me from time to time. He'd call now and then to ask if I needed anything, and he came to Atlanta and we'd spend the day together. It was... nice, you know?"

I nodded and let her continue.

"I was living on my own, and he knew how alone I felt down there in Georgia. It wasn't until last year that we... Only last year, really..."

Her voice trailed off and her eyes brimmed with tears.

"So... only last year," she continued. "But it was nice. He came down to see me and we had a great time. I never came here because he was worried about it."

"Why was that?" I asked.

"Well, making this video, knowing about some of the creeps and dangerous people that come around his bar, Dad thought it was best for people not to know about me."

She gave me a small smile. "It hurt my feelings at first. For a while I wondered if it was because he was ashamed of me. He never spent any time with me when I was growing up... And when we got to talking after my mom passed, it felt like maybe he was just being nice. It wasn't until a few months ago that I began to believe he wasn't, that he really cared. He told me he regretted all the time he wasted, all the time he could've spent with me."

I kept my expression neutral. What she was telling me was a surprise, but I believed her. It wasn't telling me a whole lot, just that Benny had a secret life and that there was a different, softer side to him. I needed more.

Benny's business practices were murky, at best, but to my knowledge he'd never done anything illegal. And nothing his daughter said made me think she was lying about who she was or her relationship with her father.

"Trish," I said. "Because of the nature of your father's death and your sudden appearance, I need to ask you some... tough questions. Is that okay?"

She nodded. "Sure, that's all right."

"What do you know about the money your father left you?"

A long pause. She frowned, straightened her back and said, "Nothing. You mean the money from his business?"

"That and the half-million from his life insurance. You're about to become a very wealthy young lady. Your father said in that video that he was planning on leaving you all his cash and what was in his bank accounts. I don't yet know about his bank accounts, but the cash... That's a large sum of money. Larger than the Sorbonne's annual income. We found a safe in his office with half a million in it."

Trish blinked. Her mouth opened. Her eyes widened. "W... W... What?"

"You heard me, and there's more. Your father was hosting poker games in a hidden room off his office. Did he ever mention that?"

"No. No, sir."

"I'm wondering if that's why he didn't want you coming here. You're sure he didn't mention it while you were recording the video?"

"No, I swear. He never told me anything about poker or... Anything."

Suddenly, her eyes grew wide, and her face flushed.

"Are you trying to say that the money my dad left me is tied up in something illegal? You think my father was some kind of criminal?" And with that she burst into tears.

"Hey, hey," I said, leaning forward and taking her hand. "It's okay. No, I don't think your father was a criminal. But we don't know where the money came from, not yet."

Trish was really... upset, crying, agitated, and I couldn't blame her. She'd said so herself that she hardly knew her father. The lack of communication and then, after only the short time he'd been in her life, he wound up dead, murdered, and now this. It would have been more than most people could have handled. To tell you the truth, I felt sorry for the girl. My mind was spinning thinking about all the possibilities, and it made me mad that this poor kid was being put through the wringer.

"Trish, look at me," I said. I was still holding her hand. She looked up at me through the tears and sobbed. "Listen to me," I continued. "I promise you I'll honor your father's wishes. Your father, Benny, and I, we didn't exactly see eye to eye sometimes, but we were friends for a lot of years. I can't promise you I'll find his killer, but I can promise you that my team and I will do our best. I hope you can believe that."

She nodded, sniffled and said, "Thank you, Mr. Starke." And she squeezed my hand.

"Call me Harry," I said. "And don't worry, Trish. I'll stay in touch. Come on. Let's get out of here."

I escorted her back to Kate's office to find that Laura had left. Kate was there, so was Mike, and so was Bill Perks, sitting in a chair at the table glued to his phone.

"Bill," I said as we stepped into the office, "Trish is ready to go. I don't think we need you for anything more right now, but I'm sure we'll be in touch."

He grunted as he stood up. The look in his beady eyes made it pretty clear he wasn't happy.

"I'll process the Sorbonne's paperwork as soon as I can and release Ms. Hinkle's inheritance, but before I can, I need a full accounting of Mr. Hinkle's assets." He turned to Mike. "When will you be releasing the building?"

Mike shrugged and said, "We're still processing it. Could be a few days, maybe a week."

That didn't go down well. Perks wasn't buying it.

"I want you to know, all of you, that I will be protecting the rights of my clients."

"Oh, we're aware," Mike replied dryly.

It never ceases to amaze me how some lawyers talk to the police as if we're stupid, as if we don't understand the law. I've met a lot of attorneys, both as a cop and as a PI. Most of them are understanding and sometimes easy to get along with. Some, though, are a royal pain in the ass. Which was my first impression of Bill Perks. Suffice it to say, I wasn't impressed and I wanted out of there.

I needed to get back to the office to see what progress my team had made, and to update them on the monkey wrench that was Trish Hinkle.

Chapter Thirteen

Tuesday Evening 6:45pm

It was dark when I left the police department that evening, and it was raining, a cold penetrating rain that could freeze the bones of a dead cow; it was depressing, as if I didn't have enough to depress me already. Fortunately, though, traffic in the city was light and I made it to my office in record time.

I found Tim still at the bridge of the *Enterprise* with his earphones on, huddled over one of a half-dozen keyboards, his face less than a foot from the screen, staring, squinting at it like a tiger peering through the brush. He was so focused he didn't even hear me enter.

"Hey! Tim! Updates?"

"Oh. Wow," he exclaimed, sliding his headphones down onto his neck. "Harry, hey. How did it go at the PD?"

"I'll tell you in a minute," I replied. "Jacque's not up front. Is anyone else still here?"

"TJ is. Last I saw, he was in the breakroom. But,

everyone else went home at five-thirty 'cause of the rain. Jacque told us to go in case it freezes, but it—"

"That's okay," I said interrupting his flow. "You can tell me all about it in a minute. I need to find TJ." But I didn't have to go anywhere. He walked by Tim's open door on his way out.

"Hey, TJ," I said. "You got a minute?"

"Sure," he said and stepped into Tim's office.

"Geez, I hate this place," he said as he threw his coat down on a chair. "It's too damn dark. How the hell you stand it, I don't know."

"Me neither," I said. "Okay, listen up..." And then I filled them in on... well, everything. And, as I listened to myself talk, I couldn't help but think just how ridiculous it all sounded.

TJ sat there with a befuddled look on his face, not saying a word, while Tim's eyes bounced back and forth between the two of us, his head shaking every so often in disbelief.

"So," Tim said when I was finished, "Benny hired you, us, before he even died, and his secret daughter helped him plan it?"

"More or less."

"That's..." he said and shook his head again, "frickin' crazy."

TJ snorted. "Geez, you'd think we'd be used to shit like this by now, but damn. Just when you think you've seen it all...."

"Wait..." Tim said and leaned back in his chair. "Do we know what Benny did before he ran the Sorbonne? Like, has he always been involved in hospitality?"

"Good question," I said. "I don't know. It's never come up."

"I'm still going through his finances," TJ said. "But, if you want I'll look into transactions in Atlanta, too. Now that I know he was visiting his daughter and all that other crazy stuff that happened, maybe we'll be able to find a connection."

"Yes, do that," I replied. "And dig deep. Who knows what we'll find next? After finding that half a mill—"

"Okay," TJ replied. "Tomorrow, okay? It's kinda nasty out there and I'd like to get home."

"Of course," I replied. "I'll see you in the morning. Be careful out there."

He nodded, but he didn't leave.

"Tim, where are you on decrypting the footage?" I asked.

"I'm going to pull another two hours here tonight, I think. Mike Willis called and told me he'd sent copies of the files to the TBI lab. I'm gonna do what I can to crack this before they do, if they do." He grinned up at me.

It was typical of Tim. He was going to work on it until he raced over the finish line first. To him it's a matter of "geek pride." Not that I'd ever complain about Tim's devotion to a tech-based task, or to me. He got the job done, and we needed a lead, like yesterday. The more time we spent floundering around, the less likely it was that we'd find our killer; you've heard of the forty-eight-hour rule, right? We were close to twenty-four hours in, and we still didn't have any leads; none, nada, zilch.

"Are we thinking the person who killed Benny was someone he knew?" TJ asked.

"Oh yes, he knew him. The fact that he anticipated his death tells us that," I replied. "Granted, he may have been concerned about the amount of money being won or, more importantly, lost, but the average poker player isn't going to make you that paranoid."

"Geez," Tim said. "It's awful when you think about it, right? I wonder if the poor guy was counting his days."

"Must be hard to live like that," TJ said. "I had times like that when I was in Nam. You never knew if the next minute was going to be your last. I need to go. I'll see you guys tomorrow. Have a good night." And with that, he grabbed his coat and left.

Me? I wasn't too far behind him. I bid Tim goodnight, thanked him for all his hard work, and made him promise he'd leave no later than nine and go home and get some sleep.

He promised, but knowing him as I did...

I was looking forward to dinner with my family. It was finally time to eat the tamales. Amanda had texted me a half-hour earlier with pictures of them going into the oven and one of her holding Jade together with Rose and Maria holding up their wine glasses.

Yes, I was looking forward to the festivities, but I was finding it hard to shut off the investigative side of my brain. And it was especially challenging because as I drove home that night, I couldn't get Trish Hinkle out of my head. My thoughts kept returning to that interview room, her face, her tears, the fact that her father had been murdered and she was alone in a strange city with no friends, no one to turn to. And I kicked myself for not making sure she had a place to stay. After all, she was the daughter of my friend and... It was Christmas.

How could I not take some of that home with me?

Chapter Fourteen

Tuesday Evening 7:30pm

I wasn't feeling too... good during the drive home that night, and not because of the filthy weather. No, I was going to have to face my wife. You see, I'd made her a promise that I'd enjoy some quality family time that Christmas, but I wasn't sure I could, not with Benny and Trish foremost in my mind. Oh, I wanted to, and was determined to try.

It was almost eight o'clock when I drove through the gate and into the garage. I took a deep breath, then opened the door that led to the kitchen and stepped inside to be greeted by Rose, my stepmother, with a hug and a kiss on the cheek. She'd just put some Harry Connick Jr. on the sound system. That meant my dad was probably over, too, so score one for lifting my spirits!

I've already mentioned Rose a couple of times. I've mentioned that she's my stepmother, and she is, but that's a little misleading. First, she's twenty years younger than my father, August. She's just four years older than me. She's a beautiful woman: tall, blond, perfect skin, perfect figure. When my father married her, some six years after my mother died, she had to endure a lot of crap, especially at the country club where the gossips proclaimed her "the quintessential trophy wife." Actually, that's the last thing she is. She is a very caring woman who loves my old man dearly, and I love her for that. She also adores Jade, and I love her for that too.

"This is the third ugly holiday sweater these crazy women have put her in," August said as I walked into the kitchen. "How are you, m'boy? Good day, I hope."

And there it was, the invitation to unload and spoil the moment. I didn't take it. Instead, I said, "Hello, Dad. Looks like you could use a drink," I said as I took Jade from him.

I held my daughter in my arms, kissed her forehead and looked at her. She struggled to get down, but I held onto her. I noticed her nose was red and she looked a little flushed.

"Has she been outside?" I asked.

Amanda hugged me and gave me a quick kiss, then took her from me. She was smiling. "Err, no," she replied. "We were finishing up some things in the kitchen and she got a tiny bit of cumin on her hand and stuck it in her mouth before we could stop her."

"No kidding," I said, accepting a drink from my father. "That gave her a surprise, I bet. I need to take a shower. I won't be long, okay?" Then I downed the whisky and handed the glass back to August.

"I'll have another one of those when I come back," I said, then I left them to it.

After a long hot shower, I dressed in a fresh pair of jeans and a white dress shirt—no tie—and joined them at the table to devour the tamales. Now, it wasn't the first time I'd eaten them, but those... wow. The chuck roast Maria had chosen was cooked to perfection, and Rose had made a cucumber salad that really hit the spot.

"We discovered that Amanda has no patience for peeling potatoes," Rose told me, chuckling as she passed me the bowl of mashed potatoes and onions.

"Well, it's so time-consuming and fiddly," Amanda countered. "And it's messy. I'm just glad I didn't add too much garlic like I did the last time."

Maria insisted there was "no such thing as too much garlic." My father agreed with her. Me? I diplomatically kept my mouth shut. And so, the evening rolled on until they started talking about their plans for Christmas Eve, just a week away.

Everyone was glad that, for once, we had the chance to spend more time together that year. August was already done for the year and looking forward to the break. Rose was happy, too, that she would have him all to herself for two whole weeks. And Maria? She had no family and was going to stay with us, as she always did. She had her own ensuite room over the garage with direct access to Jade's room. And that left only me. I intended to work through the 23rd, so I was the exception, but that was nothing new.

"You *will* be home for the festivities, won't you, Harry?" Maria asked.

"So long as I'm not caught up in something dire," I said as I started on my fourth tamale.

"I hope so," Maria replied. "Jade shouldn't miss out on both parents celebrating Christmas with her."

"I wouldn't miss it for the world," I said. And, I meant it. I was looking forward to a break as much as anyone, but somehow, from the silence the statement was greeted with, I got the idea that nobody believed me.

The silence lasted a few minutes—everyone was still eating—until August broke it by saying, "It's sad Benny's family has to go through this, especially now."

Again, I held my tongue, as did everyone else around the table.

Amanda twirled her wine glass between her finger and thumb, then shot me a look and rolled her eyes.

I took a deep breath. I wanted to quash the topic before it took off.

"Yes, it's sad, all right, but maybe this isn't the time to discuss it."

Maria took a sip of wine and patted my hand. "It's okay to miss him and to be sad he's gone. I understand, Harry."

She could see I didn't have anything to say so she kept going.

"We all have our own ways of looking at the world and deciding what is good and what is bad, no?" she continued. "But even bad people can be dear to you if you look beyond what you've been told to see."

August laughed and asked if she wrote holiday cards. Maria smiled and shrugged.

"When I was a little girl, I lived in a neighborhood with a lot of thugs," she said. "There was a man people talked about all the time. His name was Elivo Torres. Sometimes he was responsible for fights, lots of money going back and forth from places you didn't want to know. People were scared of him. He was like a real mob boss, you know? Like the men we see on TV. But he also did what he had to do to take care of the little people. And for that, a lot of people respected him. Sometimes life is complicated. People are complicated."

I couldn't help but agree with her. People are complicated and almost always never what they appear to be.

Benny was never my best friend, not by any standard, but he was there for me in his own sweaty, nasty way.

"You're right, Maria," I said and poured her more wine. Then, I reached over and rubbed Amanda's shoulder.

"Benny was a strange cat," I said. "At first glance he was someone you'd take an instant dislike to, as I did when I first set eyes on him all those years ago when I was a rookie cop. But then, as you got to know him, he kind of grew on you... No, he wasn't the kind of guy you invited to eat Christmas dinner with you, but he was... he was all right."

Rose coughed. August chuckled. Amanda patted my arm.

It was all true; at least to me, it was. I had no illusions about Benny. Was he a crook? Probably not, but he was a shady character and yet, that fat little man had a way of making you smile.

"He has a daughter," I told them, my jaw tightening.

Rose clicked her tongue and said, "Poor thing."

"Benny has a daughter?" Amanda said, her eyes wide.

Oh hell, I thought, *here we go.*

I spent the next several minutes giving them the short version of what had happened that afternoon. The reaction around the table was one of incredulity.

"Poor kid," Maria said when I finished.

"It is sad," Amanda said matter-of-factly. "If she is indeed his daughter. Has anyone proven that yet?"

"Proven it?" I replied. "No, of course not. It's too soon. We only met her this afternoon, but she's his daughter, all right. I'm certain of it. Okay, that's enough. I don't want to talk about it anymore. It's Christmas. Let's talk about happier things."

And we did.

It was a little after eleven that night when August and

Rose left. Maria said goodnight and went to her room. Amanda and I peeked in on Jade. She was sleeping soundly. And we went to bed.

I'd been lying in bed for nearly an hour, staring up at the ceiling. The shadow monster that lived in the corner didn't show that night, but I couldn't sleep. Benny, the card table, the safe, the camera, Trish and a host of other case-related things kept spinning through my mind.

Finally, I couldn't take it anymore. Benny's murder was haunting me. I got up to get a drink of water from the bathroom, and when I came back, the bedside lamp was on.

Amanda was sitting up on her arm looking sleepily at me.

"Can't sleep?" she asked.

"No." I sighed. "Go back to sleep." I kissed her head and turned off the lamp. I put on a pair of jeans, a T-shirt and a sweater and went out to the pool.

The rain had stopped and the sky had cleared. It was a moonless night and the city below was a fairytale world of twinkling lights. I sat on the wall for a few moments, then decided to go for a drive, so I grabbed a jacket and my trusty CZ75 and headed out into the neighborhood, taking in the Christmas lights and the trees in the front windows.

It wasn't enough. I looked at the clock on my dash. It read twelve-thirty-five.

I hope Tim went home, I thought pensively. *Hmm...*

And then I turned left onto Ochs Highway and headed downtown.

Chapter Fifteen

Wednesday Morning 12:30am

I hadn't planned to visit the Sorbonne that evening, but suddenly there I was, sitting out front in my car. It looked somehow... abandoned, a ghost of the bar it used to be. On any given day, even at that late hour, people were usually packed inside, noisy, drinking, hogging the stools.

All the lights were off. Police tape crisscrossed the entrance. I drove around to Prospect Street. The rear door was also taped and locked. Not a deterrent to someone like me. I took my trusty lockpick set from my pocket and had that door open in seconds.

It was dark inside. I closed the door silently and fumbled around for a light switch.

Damn it. Why didn't they put a switch by the door? It's like a tomb in here.

I wrestled my iPhone out of my pants pocket—I had it on silent—and turned on the flashlight. The air smelled of cigarette smoke and stale beer. *Still, no frickin' switch...*

Thud!

What the hell?

Yeah, right! What the hell? The place was supposed to be empty, and I knew as sure as hell I didn't make the noise. It came from somewhere else in the building. It sounded like it came from one of the back rooms, like Benny's office two doors up on the left.

I inched slowly forward. I was almost there when the light of another flashlight bounced quickly in and out of the hallway.

Easy, Harry, I thought as I continued my slow approach. *Whoever's holding that flashlight is moving around. Sounds like they're searching the place. Who the hell could it be?*

It couldn't have been Laura. If she'd come in to get something, she would've turned on the lights. Whoever it was either didn't know where the light switches were or they didn't want to draw attention to themselves. I opted for the latter.

I paused, drew my CZ and listened. I didn't need to check the load. I knew it was already cocked and loaded. Experience and training dictate that if you need to work the action on your firearm, you might as well be carrying a rolled-up newspaper for all the good it will do. In the time it takes to jack the slide, you could be dead.

Anyway, I strained my ears, trying to figure out what was going on. The light was indeed coming from inside Benny's office. I pocketed my phone and gripped my weapon with both hands. Then, I leaned my back against the wall and crept slowly toward the open door.

I was breathing deeply, controlling every breath, in and out. The CZ felt warm in my hands. I had my finger off the trigger, for two reasons: One, it's what you're supposed to do, and two, the trigger pull is only two-point-two pounds.

Most handgun triggers are weighted to five pounds or more. I managed to creep the rest of the way to Benny's office in silence until I saw the beam of the flashlight and froze. The intruder went quiet and turned off their light.

Damn! Now what?

I stepped up to the open doorway and tried to peer inside...

Bang! The muzzle flash blinded me for several seconds. I felt the wind of the bullet as it flew past my right ear and impacted the wall behind me. I stepped back and blinked several times. I dropped low, leaned around the doorframe and fired at the point where the muzzle blast came from. Then, knowing my assailant could only move to his right, I adjusted my aim and fired again, then again. The three shots were only nanoseconds apart. On the third shot, I heard a yelp, and someone rushed out into the hallway, knocking me sideways. I was already in a crouching position and the impact knocked me flying. I banged my head against the wall, rolled, and came into a firing position just in time to see the rear door closing, the sliver of light shrinking until it was gone altogether.

"Damn it!" I yelled as I staggered to my feet and ran to the door just in time to see a pair of taillights disappear around the corner.

"Damn it all to hell!" I said as I leaned against the doorjamb. "At least I managed to hit the bastard," I muttered. "Shit!"

I took out my phone, turned on the flashlight and found the light switch halfway up the hallway, between Benny's office and the main bar.

I angrily sat down in the chair in front of Benny's desk and flexed my hand. I'd fallen on it, as well as banging my head, and it hurt like hell. I flopped my wrist up and down.

It didn't feel broken. *Way to go, Harry,* I thought. *You really do have a knack for getting yourself tangled up... Still, I did manage to wing the bastard.*

Was it even a good thing I'd been there at that late hour? Maybe. I'd stopped the intruder from collecting whatever it was they were looking for, but a fat lot of good that did me since I hadn't managed to catch them. I didn't even know if the perp was a man or a woman.

I got up from the chair and took a good look around the office. All of Benny's desk drawers were open. A box of files from one of his shelves had been knocked over. *Must have been when I shot him.* And the door to the hidden poker room was open.

Did Mike's team leave it that way?

I knew I had to call Kate. I took a deep breath and dialed her number. The phone rang four times before she picked up.

Damn it. She must be asleep. I braced myself. She was, and she sounded annoyed.

"Harry, it's almost one-thirty."

"Kate, I'm at the Sorbonne and—"

"You've got to be kidding—"

"Someone was here," I said, interrupting her. "They broke into the bar. Front or back door, I don't know. They were looking for something in Benny's office. Whoever it was shot at me. I'm okay, but I did hit him... or her. But whoever it was got away, out the back door."

"Wait, what?"

"I don't know, Kate. Look, I didn't get the chance to see who it was."

"Stay right there, Harry. I'll be there as soon as I can with backup."

And with that, she hung up. I went out into the bar area

and busied myself looking for light switches. I found them behind the bar and turned them on. Then I checked all the windows. None of them had been broken. There was no sign of forced entry. I guess whoever it was did what I did and picked the lock.

I knew Kate's backup would be there before she was, so I went back to Benny's office and sat in the chair. I didn't know where I'd shot the person, but a gunshot wound wouldn't be easy to hide.

Did it bring us any closer to finding out who it was? Maybe. Maybe not!

Chapter Sixteen

Wednesday Morning 1am

Kate arrived some fifteen minutes later looking like she'd swallowed a pint of vinegar. The first thing she did was ask for my gun. I sucked it up and handed it to her. I've lost count of how many times that's happened.

While she and her two cops, Bert and Nicole, if I remember rightly, looked around the Sorbonne, I texted Amanda letting her know that everything was okay and I'd be home soon. Then, I joined Kate and the two officers in Benny's office.

"We found a bullet in the wall out in the hall," Kate said. "I guess that's the one he shot at you. There's one in the paneling here." Kate pointed to it. "There's another over there and a third here." She pointed to a file cabinet on the east wall, the one with the pizza boxes stacked on top of it. The top drawer had a neat round hole in it. "There are drops of blood on the floor in there and on the doorknob leading out onto Prospect Street."

"Yes," I said. "I figured I'd only clipped whoever it was. What about the bullet?"

"We'll have to let the techs figure that out. I've called it in and requested CSI. Hey," she said to one of the cops. "I'll take it from here. You two can go on back to whatever it was you were doing, but thanks for getting here as quick as you did."

He nodded, told her goodnight, gave me a half salute and together, they left.

"So, the guy," I said. "Or woman—it was dark and happened so fast I couldn't tell which—is walking around with a bullet wound. I'm betting they don't go to the hospital."

"It depends how bad the wound is," Kate replied. "There's not a whole lot of blood, but I can have someone check the hospitals and walk-in clinics. Did you see anything at all, Harry?" She blinked and rubbed her eyes. "What they were wearing? Anything?"

I racked my brain. "A hooded jacket... maybe, but most people are wearing those. It's that time of year. Sorry, Kate."

I went to the door of the secret room. It was open.

"Kate," I called over my shoulder. "Did Mike's people leave this room open?"

She stepped up beside me and said, "No... at least I don't think so."

"Well, whoever the intruder was knew it was here. Who the hell knew about it, Kate? How many people knew about it? If we can figure that out, we'll have a viable list of suspects. Until then... we've got nothing. We need that footage. Without it, we may never know."

We closed the door and slid the file cabinet back in place. Then I turned to look at the desk. The desk drawers were all open. The desktop was strewn with papers and...

"What the hell's that?" I said as I stepped closer.

In the middle of the desktop, half hidden by the papers, was another small, square camera, a twin to the one Tim was working on, only it had been smashed.

"I heard a thump almost immediately after entering through the back door," I said. "I was still in the hallway. Must have disturbed them. This camera must've been hidden somewhere in this office, and hidden well, because Mike's people didn't find it."

I looked around the room, searching for somewhere the camera might have been hidden. At first, I saw nothing. Then I spotted a free-standing cupboard to the left of the office door, tall and slim, a chimney cupboard, I think they call them. It wasn't an antique, but it looked to me like it was a custom job.

I stepped up to it. The two full-length doors were closed. I pulled them open. It was filled with... geez, I don't know. Boxes of coffee, paper plates, paper bowls, plastic cups and... well, you get the idea. I looked in the two top front corners: nothing, and then I noticed something. I closed the lefthand door and looked at the hinges. There were six of them, three to each door, big black things screwed to the outside of the door and the frame; six screws to each hinge. Sure enough, the top hinge on the lefthand door had a screw missing. If you weren't looking for it, you'd never notice the small black hole.

I opened the door again and there it was on the inside of the door, a small hole right where the back of the hinge was. I ran the tips of my fingers over the spot. It was sticky.

I went back to the desk, took a business card from my wallet and used it to lift the edge of the camera. It wouldn't move. It was stuck to the desktop.

"Yep," I said. "It was stuck to the inside of the cupboard

door. See that?" I pointed to a small, round protuberance. "That's the lens. It would have been pushed into the hole."

"So they came to collect the cameras, then," Kate said. "If so, they must have been highly pissed when they found the one in the poker room was missing."

"Whoever it was must have panicked when they heard me out in the hallway and smashed this one," I said.

She nodded thoughtfully, took an evidence bag from her pocket, opened it and slipped it over the broken camera without touching it with her fingers. Then, gripping it through the bag, she picked it up. It came away with a sticky, ripping sound. She shook it into the bag, closed it, signed and dated it, then shoved it into her jacket pocket.

"Why didn't he just take it with him?" she mused.

"Maybe he was going to but dropped it when I shot him." I shrugged.

Kate heaved a deep breath and shook her head. "Maybe we'll get lucky and find some prints on it," she said. "I doubt we'll get anything from the camera itself, but you never know."

I was still perusing the room, checking for anything else the intruder might have moved or been looking for.

Kate continued, "Mike's people will be back here in the morning. I think we're done here for now, don't you?" Kate looked at her watch. "Geez, it's almost two-thirty... Harry, what were you doing here?"

"You know, I really don't know. I couldn't sleep so I went for a drive and somehow ended up here. Gut feeling, I suppose."

"That gut of yours is going to get you killed one of these days," she replied.

I shrugged.

"I'm going home, Harry. You should too. You look like

shit. Go home. Get some sleep. We need you at the top of your game. Does Amanda know where you are? Of course she doesn't. Go on, get out of here."

She gave me that old familiar "Kate" look. I smirked.

"Yes, ma'am," I said.

She grimaced but didn't protest.

It was just after three when I finally arrived home. The streets were deserted, so I had an easy drive. I was exhausted, so I took my time.

I tiptoed through the house, trying not to make a noise. I didn't want to wake Amanda or Jade, but it wasn't just that. As late as it was, I felt that electric jitter coursing through my body: the adrenaline of a near miss in a gunfight hadn't worn off.

It was the craziest thing: Only a few hours ago I'd enjoyed a nice dinner with my family, then, less than an hour later, someone had nearly shot my ear off. You don't come down from something like that quickly, or easily.

So I kicked off my shoes onto the mat in the hall, hung up my coat, and tiptoed into the living room. I didn't turn on the lights. I didn't need to. There was enough coming from our tree; more than enough for me to find my way around the coffee table to the liquor cabinet, where I found a glass and a half-empty bottle of macadamia nut whiskey. It was a gift from someone—I don't remember who—two Christmases earlier. Not what I usually drink, but it was wet, fiery and had a strangely satisfying taste.

I poured just a little into the glass. *No need to go crazy. You have to get up in the morning.*

The sofa welcomed me into its arms. I heaved a huge sigh... Of relief? Perhaps, but maybe there was more to it. I gulped down the whiskey, chilled by the realization that I'd likely been in the same room as the person who shot Benny to death. And whoever it was had tried to kill me too, but what was worse was the realization that I might not be able to find the killer.

My wrist was still sore from the fall. I massaged it gently, hoping it would feel better by the morning.

You're getting old, Harry. You think?

I finished my whiskey, too run down to hold on to the anger. I left the glass on the coffee table and went to bed.

Amanda was sound asleep. I didn't need to turn on the light. I knew my way around the bedroom. I knew what she looked like, curled up under the covers. I stood for a moment, then shed my clothes and climbed in beside her. I wrapped my arms around her and pulled her in close. Though still asleep, she relaxed into my hug and I buried my face in her hair. The feel of her and the scent of her gave me the rush of comfort I needed. I was home again with the woman I love asleep in my arms.

And with one final sigh of relief, I fell sound asleep.

Chapter Seventeen

Wednesday Morning 8:30am

I slept late that morning. It was almost eight-thirty when I finally made it to the shower. Amanda was up and about doing something with Maria and Jade in the kitchen. I was just drying off when my phone rang. It was Tim.

"Hey, Tim," I said. "You're early. What's up?"

"Harry. Hope I haven't caught you at a bad time."

"Nope. I'm just running a little late, is all. What do you need?"

"I finally managed to get through the encryption and I was able to retrieve the footage. I sent a copy to the PD, as they said, and I kept two copies for us. I need to take you through it. How long before you get here?"

"Well done, son. I knew you could do it. I'll be there as soon as I can—an hour, maybe less. In the meantime I'll call Kate. You have Jacque, TJ and Heather be in the conference room at say..." I looked at the bedside clock, then continued, "nine-fifteen."

"Okay... You're not going to like it, Harry."

"Tim, there's a lot about this case I don't like. Why would things change now? Don't worry. I'll be there as soon as I can."

I hung up, called Kate, asked her to join us, finished dressing and headed to the kitchen. I needed coffee in the worst way.

"Morning, hon," Amanda said and handed me a cup of coffee. "I figured you could use one of these."

I kissed her on the forehead. "One? I need more than that today." I took a sip. "Thank you."

"So what happened last night? Where were you?"

I shared only what I had to with her, sparing her the gruesome details. It wasn't the time to worry her. Amanda is one of the most resilient people I know, but knowing I'd almost walked into a death trap wasn't something she'd take lightly. I'd tell her, of course, but at a time when I wasn't in a rush. Luckily, she didn't ask too many questions. So, after I downed my cup of coffee, she made me another to-go, and I was ready to hit the road and as ready as I'd ever be to face the day, whatever it might hold for me.

"I'll try to get home early, I promise," I told her as she and Maria prepped Jade for a day of last-minute Christmas shopping.

Amanda gave me an "I'll believe it when I see it" smile.

"Trust me," I replied. "I need to catch up on sleep."

Kate was getting out of her car when I pulled into the parking lot at the office. She had Samson in the back seat of the car. I told her, rather than leave him out there in the cold, to bring him into the office, and she did.

She looked at me and shook her head.

"What?" I asked.

"You look like shit. Your eyes look like pee holes in the

snow... you look like a damn zombie."

"Geez, thanks for the kind words," I said. "You don't look so great yourself." Actually, she did. She always does. "Anybody would think you'd been up all night."

She snorted. I followed her through the front door and on to the conference room, where we found the rest of the players waiting for us.

Tim was front and center, trying to connect his laptop to the new wall monitor.

"Sorry, Harry," he said, looking round at me, "I should have set this up earlier. I need a different cable. I'll be right back." And with that he scurried to his office.

By then, Samson had made the rounds, saying hello to everyone before Kate sat down with him on a short leash and he settled down beside her.

"Umm, while we're waiting for Tim," TJ said. "I have some news about Benny's financial records."

"Let's hear it, then," Jacque said.

TJ nodded and passed a stack of papers to Heather, who separated them and gave one set to Kate, one to Jacque and one to me. On the top sheet was a list of bank accounts, all in Benny's name.

"From the looks of it," TJ said, "Benny Hinkle was into something big. Those accounts are just the ones I could find so far. I have a feeling he has more offshore. I'm still working on that. But those you have in your hands total just over two million dollars. And you say you found another half-million in his safe. He also moved it around a lot. You have all the dates there, but it looks like it was this fall when he made most of the transfers or withdrawals."

"Geez," I said. "Two and a half million. What the hell was he doing? How could he have made that kind of money? The Sorbonne was doing well... but not that well."

"That's a good question," Kate said.

I looked around the room. No one had any ideas. It was then I took the opportunity to tell everyone what had happened over the last forty-eight hours, letting Kate jump in whenever she felt the need to paint a more complete picture.

"Frickin' hell, Harry," TJ said. "You're lucky you weren't killed."

TJ was very protective of me. Kate found him on the streets, homeless and ready to cash in his chips; that is until he discovered the body of a young woman in a back alley. Kate was the investigating officer and she saw something in him nobody else did, so she brought him to me. It turned out he's a highly decorated Vietnam vet—two tours, one in 1968 and another in 1972—a retired Marine down and out, the victim of a shady bank officer who framed him for stealing from the bank. He didn't do it. He did some time, and it ruined him. He lost everything: wife, kids, home. He has a degree in accounting, and at the time, I was looking for a financial investigator. So, bearing in mind the man's military record, including his Silver Star and two Purple Hearts, I figured I'd take a chance. So I hired him. At sixty-eight, he's the oldest member of my team. He's also a stone-cold killer. He'll kill at the drop of a hat. I know, I've seen him do it. Something he'd picked up in Nam, I guess. But never talks about it. He's six feet tall, one-hundred-ninety pounds, with white hair and a heavily lined, deeply tanned face.

"I've had worse days, TJ," I replied. "You of all people should know that."

He opened his mouth again to speak, then shook his head and changed his mind.

Jacque snorted angrily, and Heather gave me a weary laugh.

"I've got it!" Tim yelled as he came rushing back into the conference room. It took him less than a minute to hook everything up and then he turned, his face beaming, but I could tell by his eyes that he'd not slept well that night either. A couple of clicks on his keyboard and he had footage queued up and ready for us to watch.

I leaned back in my chair and blinked several times. My eyes felt dry and itchy, due to lack of sleep, I supposed.

"I'm sorry, there won't be any audio." Tim shook his head apologetically. "I did everything I could, but I just wasn't able to save it. I'll keep trying, but without the encryption key, I doubt I'll be able to rescue what's being said."

"Don't worry about it, Tim," Kate said. "We sent a copy over to the local TBI office. They did a rush decryption, but they got nothing, not even video. They emailed me this morning saying it wasn't viewable, and they were grateful you sent them what you had."

His shoulders relaxed as he smiled. "Well, that's nice to hear, I guess."

"Whatever you got, Tim, is probably all we'll get... and that reminds me..." I told them about the second camera we'd found in Benny's office. Tim offered to take a look at it. Kate told him she'd have it sent over as soon as Mike's tech had finished with it.

"I do have some good news, though," Tim said. "I found footage of both the office and the poker room on this one camera. He must have been in the habit of moving it from one room to the other as needed. Maybe that second camera wasn't working."

"Really," I said, feeling a slight headache coming on. "That's terrific. Let's see it."

Chapter Eighteen

Wednesday Morning 9:45am

Tim, remote in hand, stood to one side, close to Samson, who licked his hand, startling him. Samson merely gazed up at him, his tongue lolling out to one side. Tim pushed his glasses further up the bridge of his nose and said, "Sorry about the sound, but the video isn't too bad."

He clicked the remote and the footage started rolling.

The scene opened with a view of the poker table. Seated around it was a surprisingly eclectic group of people.

"Freeze that, Tim," I said, leaning forward. And he did.

Benny was at the center facing the camera. He was dealing cards and talking. Yes, I know the screen was frozen but believe me, he was talking. His overall posture and demeanor was that of someone who was on edge. Why wouldn't he be? He was sitting next to a criminal.

Franco de Luca, Sal de Luca's younger brother, was playing, frozen in the act of throwing a chip on the table. *What the hell was Benny thinking?* I wondered.

"Are you seeing what I'm seeing?" TJ growled.

"Not the cream of Chattanooga society, is it?" I replied without taking my eyes off the screen.

All six seats were occupied. The players included Benny, five men and one woman. At first, I thought I didn't know any of them except Benny and de Luca, but I was wrong.

"Okay," I said. "Roll it."

Most players were staring at the cards, maintaining stony faces as Benny passed out the final round of cards. One of the larger guys was leaning back smoking a cigarette, a dour expression on his face, but he looked kind of familiar.

"I know that guy," Kate said, leaning forward and pointing to him. "That one, on the right, there. Isn't that Rod Harris?"

Rod Harris?

"Harry, you and I put him away. Remember? Back in oh-seven, I think it was."

Rod Harris used to be a cop, one of Chattanooga's finest... Or should I say worst? We'd arrested him a long while ago for shaking down prostitutes. He and another cop were operating their own private protection racket. I looked at the timestamp of the footage on the corner of the screen. It was shot two weeks earlier.

"This is recent," I said.

"He's been out on parole for about three months," Kate said, rolling her eyes.

It was never a cakewalk putting another officer away. I'm sure she was getting heated seeing this man potentially already involved in another crime.

Benny was sitting to Franco de Luca's right. Each time I saw that man's face, he looked more and more like a vulture. His eyes looked hollow because of the way the overhead light, the only light in the room, cast shadows on his eye sockets. He looked like a ghoul.

Sitting to Benny's right was another guy I thought looked familiar. It took me a minute, but then I got it: the guy used to run with Shady Tree. At the time, I didn't know his name, but I did recognize his face.

"Three out of six, then," Jacque said, "and we've had a problem with all three of them," she pointed out. She winced, watching the poker game begin to unfold. "What was Benny doing getting mixed up with this lot?"

"It's like the Legion of Doom," Tim joked.

I glanced around the circle. No one knew what he was talking about.

"The Legion of Doom?" Heather asked.

"You know," Tim cracked a small smile and shrugged. "From the Super Friends! They're your Rogues Gallery."

"Apparently," I replied.

"Does anyone recognize the other two?" TJ asked.

I shook my head as I stared at the Latino man sitting to Franco's left. His head was shaved and he had a goatee. I figured he was probably in his mid-to-late forties. He looked familiar, but I couldn't put a name to him. Maybe it was just that I'd seen so many criminals like him before. Maybe it was the body language. He was wearing a leather jacket, jeans and heavy boots. He was leaning back in his chair with his arms folded across his chest. Or, maybe it was just because he looked like bad news.

The woman? I certainly didn't know her. She was older and she was sitting to Shady Tree's henchman's left, her back straight, stiff, like a board. I figured she was probably in her early sixties. She frowned throughout the video, her lips almost always pursed tightly: her version of a poker face, I assumed. She wore her graying hair swept up in a bun. She looked gaunt, but I think that was because the harsh light certainly did her no favors. But I'd learned many times over the years not to judge a person on the strength of their appearance alone.

The final player in the game was also the youngest. Either that or he took very good care of himself. He couldn't have been much more than thirty. He was leaning on the table with confidence. His dark eyes shifted from player to player, like a shark circling the waters. His jet black hair was cut close to his head, like that of a Marine. The difference was that his was left long on the top. His features were... sharp: thin nose, thin lips, bony cheeks.

Yes... that's an awful lot of confidence for such a young face.

"Ideas, anyone?" I asked as the video ended. I looked around the table.

No one spoke. Jacque and Heather shook their heads. TJ simply shrugged. Samson snapped his jaws.

Tim closed the window on his laptop and pulled up a half-dozen screenshots of the individual poker players.

"Now," he said. "based on other clips I watched, these are his regulars. Here are hard copies for you all." He handed them out.

"Thanks, Tim," I said. "Good job."

I got up from my seat and stepped over to the screen, rotating my wrist. The pain was subsiding, thankfully.

"So," I said, "these six people are our prime suspects. Two of them we know for certain. Franco de Luca and Rod Harris." I pointed to each of them in turn. "This one worked for Shady Tree. We don't know his name, but we can easily find out. The other three... Tim, we need to figure out who they are and track them down."

TJ rubbed his hands together. Kate and Jacque sat up

straighter, Heather picked up her pen and Samson sat up, panting.

Me? I was excited. Now we had something to work with, someone to talk to.

"Tim, I want you to go through every piece of footage we have. You said these people are all regulars?"

"Yes. The camera seems to have been moved back and forth between the poker room and Benny's office. There are a total of eight games over ten weeks. They all played just about every week. Not always on the same day, but once a week. Oh, and here's the weird thing: the games never lasted more than a couple of hours. They started around nine and were always finished before midnight. Don't poker games usually go on all night? That's what I've heard... anyway."

"You've been watching too many movies, Tim," I said and smiled. But I knew he was right. Two hours is hardly worth sitting down for, which meant... what? Inwardly, I shook my head, then continued.

"So, this is the pattern we'll follow. Heather, I want you and Tim to review the footage of all eight games and do what you can to identify the three people we don't know. The older woman, the young man with black hair, and the guy with the goatee. I want their information and their last known whereabouts."

Heather nodded, scribbling furiously on her paper.

"Tim, get Heather started on the footage. Then I want you to go through Benny's cell phone. He had to have been communicating with these people to set up the games. I want phone numbers, text messages and voice mails. Got it?"

"Yes, sir."

"TJ. You keep digging into Benny's finances. I'd like to

know who those big transfers were going to and where the deposits were coming from. See if you can dig up anything on offshore or shell accounts... Hell, I don't need to tell you how to do your job."

TJ grinned at me and nodded.

"Kate," I said, turning to her. "Can you find out where Rod Harris is now? If he's on parole, he has to be in town somewhere. We already know where de Luca is. The other guy, the one who worked for Shady, he shouldn't be too difficult to track. He should have a rap sheet, right?"

She nodded, then said, "Rod Harris is the easy one." She took out her phone. "I'll contact the parole office right now and then we'll go and have a little chat with him."

She dialed the number then, while it was ringing, she said, "I'll have Corbin pull Shady's records. There should be something there... Hello, yes. This is Captain Gazzara, CPD. I need to know where one of your parolees is. His name is Rodney Harris. He was paroled about three months ago... Yes, I'll wait. Thank you... That was quick..." She wrote something down in her notepad, then said thank you again and hung up.

She looked at me, smiled and said, "Got it. He works at a mechanic shop on Rossville Boulevard."

"Do we think any of these people had access to the poker room?" TJ asked. "I know you said it was accessible by key, but d'you think anyone might have had copies?"

Good question, I thought. Then, I thought back to what had happened last night.

"The room was supposed to be kept locked, Kate. Isn't that correct?" I asked.

"Yes," she replied. "But it was open last night. So either Benny kept a spare key hidden somewhere in his office and Mike's people didn't find it, or someone had a copy."

"It's possible they all had keys," I said, "but not likely. Benny was a fussy little... He wouldn't have handed out keys to all and sundry. Not only are these six individuals our best bets for Benny's murder, but there's a good chance one of them was at the Sorbonne last night."

I wracked my brain again, trying to remember the build of the person who attacked me. The only person I could confidently rule out was the woman.

"I don't think she was there last night," I said, pointing to her image on the screen. "But that doesn't mean she isn't involved in Benny's murder. In fact, any one of them, or all of them, could've wanted him dead."

Kate nodded. "I think we should talk to his daughter again, Harry. It's probably a long shot, but he might've mentioned a name or told her something that could help us."

"That's true," I said. "Okay, everyone. You have your assignments. Let's go to it."

And with that, I cut everyone loose. They practically marched out of the conference room, a sight that had me feeling much better about things, though I still had that something nagging away at me deep in my gut.

Kate took Samson out to her car while I went to the coffee machine. I needed another cup in the worst way. The thought of that and the buttered pecan creamer almost made me giddy. I snagged two to-go mugs—Kate would certainly appreciate some joe for the road—and set the coffee machine working. It slurped and whirred as it did its thing. I closed my eyes, worked my jaw, and remembered Benny's message.

Don't worry, Benny. We're on it. We will find the bastard who killed you.

That... I promise.

Chapter Nineteen

Wednesday Morning 11am

"**D**id you know Rod Harris was out on parole?" I asked as we drove to Rossville Boulevard.

It was a cold and gloomy day, raining again, just depressing, and it was cooling down with freezing rain in the forecast. We'd had to run to the car. We had the heater on and our coffees in hand. The rain pelted us as we turned off I-24 onto the ramp and I wondered if maybe the universe was trying to wake us up so we could chase down Benny's killer.

"I do remember hearing about it, Harry," Kate replied. "I remember it coming across my desk. I didn't think too much of it at the time... You know how that is, right? I meant to tell you, but what with Thanksgiving—and the Father Doberczec case—well, I just forgot about it. You know I wouldn't be here but for Samson, don't you?"

Kate sipped her coffee and looked sideways at me. I looked around. Samson was sitting up looking between us out through the windshield, panting.

"Good boy, Samson," I said and was rewarded with a snap of his jaws.

"Yes, I heard," I said. "Your good deed paid off big time."

"You mean adopting him? Yes, I suppose so," she said as she turned right onto Rossville Boulevard. "When I first got him, I was worried I wouldn't be able to handle him; he's so big. But you wouldn't believe how well trained he is. He even talks to me. Listen. Speak to me Samson."

"Woof," and he snapped his jaws.

I could feel his hot breath on my neck.

"Amazing," I said, for want of something else to say. "I think... we're almost there. It should be down there on the right, maybe a half-mile or so."

"Geez," she said, leaning forward to peer out of the windshield. "It always seems to pour around the holidays. By the way, did you get a gift for Amanda yet?"

I snorted. "Not hardly. I haven't had time."

"Oh, don't give me that. Make time, Harry."

"Easy for you to say," I replied. "What do you get for a woman who says she doesn't want anything?"

I turned to look at her. She smiled and shook her head. "That's something you'll have to work out for yourself."

"I asked her for a list," I said, "but she just shrugged and said, 'I have everything I need right here.' She was holding Jade, of course... so what the hell do I do? I want to get her something nice, you know?"

Kate smiled at me and drank more of her coffee. "Buy her a massage or something. A day at the spa."

"Massage? Spa?"

"She had to do all that physical therapy, right, after she got hurt? And, she's taking care of your eighteen-month-old baby and your parents for Christmas. Tell me she wouldn't love a chance to take a breather and get herself pampered. That's what I'd want."

"Good point, Kate... Okay. I'll think about it."

We were looking for a mechanic shop somewhere on the right. Thinking about Rod Harris being out and about was souring my already somber mood. Not that I'd started the day off peppy to begin with.

"I can't believe Franco de Luca was at that table," I said.

"Me neither," Kate said.

"Wasn't he supposed to be locked up too?"

"I don't think so," she replied. "He's slick as a snake, is that one, but I haven't heard anything bad about him; not lately, anyway. Then again, people like de Luca have a habit of slipping through the cracks."

I nodded, but said nothing. His elder brother, Sal de Luca, was... as bad as they come. Franco was no better.

"Well, whatever," Kate said, "we need to talk to him." She took another quick sip of her coffee and set the cup down in the cup holder. I did the same.

"You're right," I said. "He's not the type to play poker. There was something else going on there. What the hell is he into? And, why the hell would Benny be around someone like that anyway?"

I must have sounded angry because Kate looked at me and said, "You need to take a breath, Harry. Before we talk to Harris. I don't want you knocking his teeth out."

"There it is," I said, pointing.

The shop, On the Go Auto, had seen better days. A concrete block-built garage with four service bays and an office, it was a dowdy-looking place. The neon sign in the office window flickered. The sign on a tall post at the front of the lot was in dire need of paint. Surprisingly, though, it was busy. The bays were full and there were a dozen or more cars in the front lot. The office door looked like it had been kicked in several times, and the entire building was in serious need of a paint job.

Leave it to Rod Harris to find himself a classy place, I thought as we exited the car.

The rain had eased up. Funny how it can be raining on one side of town and not the other.

Kate put Samson on his leash and together, the three of us approached the first bay where we could see a mechanic working under the hood of a sixty-six Chevy Chevelle. I asked him where we could find Rod Harris.

"Bay four," he answered and pointed.

"Harry frickin' Starke," Harris said when he saw us. "And his trusty sidekick, Kate Gazzara. Frickin' hell. What am I supposed to have done this time?"

Kate glared at him. Samson took a step forward and he wasn't smiling. Kate pulled him back and said, "Easy, Sam... We're not here to arrest you, Rod," she said as he came out from under the car he was working on. "But, we are here to ask you some questions."

"Sure you are," he replied dryly. "Let's go to the office. It's more private there."

The office was, I expected, typical of the brand: dusty, cluttered and depressing.

"Sit down," he said as he sat down behind his desk and leaned back and laced his fingers together in his lap.

Harris is a big man, all of two-fifty and fit. He was, I knew, forty-eight years old, but he looked older. His face was tanned, his hair a dirty gray, and he looked tired.

"Well, look at you both," he said when we were settled. "Kate, you haven't changed a bit in the last twelve years. You always were a good-lookin' broad. I used to envy you, you know, Harry. We all knew you two were at it. And you,

you son of a bitch, Starke. You owe me for the last twelve years. And what's with the puppy, Kate? They demote you to dog catcher?"

At that last one, I couldn't help myself. I had to laugh.

"Shut the hell up for a moment, Rod," I said, "and listen. What do you know about Benny Hinkle's murder?"

"Hah! Is that what this is about? What do I know? I know nothing, except that someone offed the fat little pig."

"Where were you on Sunday evening between seven and nine?" Kate asked.

He looked at her and said, "Where was I? It was Sunday. I was home."

"Can anyone corroborate that?" she asked.

"No! I was there alone, thanks to you two. My wife divorced me ten years ago. Now I live alone like a frickin' hermit."

"Do you like to play poker, Rod?" I asked.

"Yeah, I play now and then."

"You played at the Sorbonne?" I asked, watching his face.

"The Sorbonne?" He shook his head. "No!" he lied.

"There you go," I said. "Now why would you lie about it? We know you were a regular at Benny's private game. We have you on video. Why the hell d'you think we're here?"

He looked stunned. He sat up in his chair, stared first at me, then at Kate and said, "I didn't kill Benny. And that's all I'm going to say." He crossed his arms again, leaned back in his chair and added, "Because I didn't."

"Did you know about the murder?" Kate asked.

"Yeah, I knew. It's all over town, damn it. I didn't off him, and I don't want you telling anyone about the games.

I'm still on parole. You know that. They find out, they'll throw me back in the can."

"We know that," Kate replied. "So why play?"

"I wanted to make some extra money," he said quietly.

"Fine," Kate said. "Tell us what was going on and I'll do my best to keep you out of trouble. But don't lie. If you do..." She didn't bother to finish the sentence. He knew what she meant. "Rod," she continued, taking out her iPad, "I'm going to record this interview. You're not under arrest. You can refuse to say anything at any time. This recording will not be used as evidence. It's for your protection as well as ours. Do you agree?"

Reluctantly, he nodded, then said yes.

"Very well," Kate said. "You may proceed. Tell us about the poker games."

"I got invited to the game through a friend of a friend," he began. "I'd been to the bar before, and with one of the first poker games I played, I made a decent chunk of change. Everybody did."

I looked at Kate, then said, "Everybody? That's not possible."

"Everyone except Benny," he replied.

It didn't make any sense.

"We bought chips from Benny and he cashed us out when the game was over." He uncrossed his arms and slipped his hands into his pants pockets. He looked nervous.

"Look, I know it seems like it was a weird setup, but I actually liked it. I enjoyed it... When I was in prison..." He swallowed. "Cops and feds... they don't fare well. You know. I can handle myself. So I did okay. I played cards to build up some cred. I just got a taste for it, is all. It was something to pass the time. That's why I went to Benny's games. That's it. I didn't kill him. I got there Sunday night around nine and the street out back was full of cop cars, fire trucks and whatever, so I turned around and high-tailed it out of there. That's it. That's all I know." He shook his head and said, "I... didn't... kill... him."

"And that's it?" Kate asked. "Why was it so difficult to tell us?"

He shrugged. "I don't know. I guess I'm worried about parole, but... Look, it was just a poker game. I know I'm not supposed to be around felons, but as far as I know, none of the other players are... felons. I always took my own money that I'd gotten from the bank. I've deposited my cash winnings. The banks never said anything. So there's nothing I've done that you can get me for."

"At least one of the players is a convicted felon," Kate said.

Harris turned a whiter shade of pale.

Benny could have been charged with organizing an illegal gambling game—just a misdemeanor—but the players? De Luca was a felon, and I was pretty sure that Shady's henchman was too. The others? I didn't know. That being so, if everything Harris told us was true, I had to wonder how Kate was going to handle his perceived parole violation. Ignorance is not an excuse under the law.

"Who would want Benny dead?" Kate asked. "Any idea? Someone who didn't play nice, maybe? How did he get along with the rest of the players?"

He shook his head and said, "I didn't kill him."

"Who were the other players, Rod?" I asked.

He stared down at the floor, shook his head and said, "I can't speak on that. I don't know any names. We used aliases with each other. Benny was Joker... There was a Latino with a beard we called Goat. A black guy we called Lefty. An I-tie we called Spaghetti. A young guy we called

Kid. A woman we called Lady. That's it. That's how it was done. All I know is, I wouldn't kill someone over a card game. Is that it? If it is, I need to get back to work. My customer will be here to get his car soon."

We pressed him for more answers, but Rod was done talking. He led us out into the shop. On the way, out of nothing but curiosity, I asked him how come he was working there.

"I own the place," he said curtly.

"You what?" Kate asked, leaning down and caressing Samson's ears.

He caught our expressions, smirked and said, "Inherited the shop from my old man. He took over this place back in '54 when he was in his early twenties. My grandpa owned the property before that, but my dad really got it going. It was the time of the hot cars, the beginnings of NASCAR, you know... moonshine runners. Did you know there used to be a racetrack on Moccasin Bend?"

I nodded. I knew it, but I didn't think Kate did because she didn't say anything.

Harris frowned, picked up a file from one of the workbenches and put it away on a shelf on the back wall.

"I never really cared much about working on cars, but I'm not going back to police work anytime soon... am I?"

He gave Kate a sharp look but didn't push his luck.

I didn't know how to feel about it. The guy was a convicted felon only lately out of prison. I almost felt sorry for him; almost, but not quite.

"You guys shut me away. My dad ran the place until he died from a heart attack, just over a year ago; then it shut down. I couldn't even go to the funeral. It stayed closed up until I got out, and now I'm running the place. I hired the first three employees this place has seen in more than a year. That's why I needed the extra money."

His tone was both bitter and sad.

"Just trying to get by around the holidays, you know?"

Kate didn't say anything. Neither of us were sure what to do with what we'd learned. I had my suspicions that there was way more to his story than he'd told us, but he wasn't budging, and I knew that grilling him more wasn't likely to get us anywhere.

I signaled to Kate that we needed to leave, and we did. But as we turned to head out into the parking area, Harris stopped us. He just needed to know.

"Hey! You guys are going to keep this under wraps for me, aren't you?"

I looked him dead in the eyes. He really had gained a lot of years while he was locked up. But he didn't just look older. He was worn down. An ex-cop, responsible for the crimes he'd committed, and now he was gambling for money with lowlifes, tucked away in a secret back room, skulking around at night like a hungry possum. He'd gone from hero to a bottom-feeder.

I bit my tongue, then said, "We'll do what we can, Rod."

He looked at Kate. She stared back at him but said nothing. He nodded. Then, before he turned away with his head down, he said, "Thank you... both."

Chapter Twenty

Wednesday Afternoon 12:15pm

Five minutes later Kate and I were pulled off on the north side of Rossville Boulevard, trying to decide where to go next.

"You know I should report him to his parole officer, right?" Kate asked. "We know de Luca's a felon, and how many of the others at that poker table are too? I don't know."

I sighed and said, "Yes. I knew you were going to bring that up. You did tell him you'd try to keep him out of trouble."

"I know what I said, but—"

"Why not cut him a break, Kate? For Pete's sake, he did almost twelve years and it does look like he's trying to make a go of the shop. So the man played a little cards to meet his payroll. So what? If he didn't know who they were..."

She thought for a moment, then sighed and said, "If he didn't. That's a big if, Harry." She shook her head, then continued. "Okay. I'll keep it to myself... if I can. But it's bound to come out. You know that."

"True, but if he is telling us the truth, I'll speak up for him. How about you?"

She thought for a minute and then said, "Deal! Now let's get back to the job at hand. Are we going to talk to de Luca?"

I knew that Tim and Heather had been searching for the identities of the four other players that morning, but I'd heard nothing from either of them. I could have called, but I knew it was pointless. If they'd found anything, they would have called me. So, since the only other player we knew for sure was Franco de Luca, it made sense to talk to him.

"What do you think?" I asked her. "Do you think we can shake some answers out of him?"

Kate didn't need to think about it. She knew de Luca as well as I did, and she didn't like him either.

"Quite frankly..." She paused then, putting the car in drive, said, "Let's go shake his tree a little; see if we can shake something loose. Though, somehow, I doubt it."

It was fifteen minutes past noon when we arrived at de Luca's Italian restaurant on Camden Street just off McCallie. Franco had taken over the business after his older brother Sal was killed by my ex-partner, Bob Ryan. Though Sal was gone, the restaurant hadn't folded. It had always been a popular eatery, and the food wasn't bad either. Not that I patronized the place; I didn't, but the locals loved it and wanted to keep the place going.

We exited the car and Kate secured Samson in the back seat and rolled the rear windows down a third of the way. I looked up at the sky.

"It's going to rain again soon," I said.

"Yes, looks like it. It'll be okay. I have a feeling we won't be in there long."

Walking into the darkened interior after more than

seven years was... underwhelming, but with a sense of déjà vu. The smell of sauce and spices washed over me like a wave.

The interior was long and narrow: a central walkway bounded by booths; eight on either side with room enough for ninety-six guests. It was a small, high-end ristorante and reservations for dinner were mandatory; lunch was first come, first served.

I said déjà vu. Oh yes. Standing at the corner of the bar, in exactly the same spot Sal used to occupy, stood Franco, his back to the bar, one foot on the brass rail, with a thug on either side of him standing like statues wearing high-dollar suits.

"I'm going to let you take the lead on this one," Kate whispered as we walked together, side-by-side, up the aisle to the bar.

"Good enough," I replied. I knew how to handle Franco. I figured that, with the right motivation, I just might get him to spill the beans.

"Well, well, look who it is. What the hell are you doing here, Harry?" Franco asked as we approached. He grinned. "It really is Christmas, seeing so many friendly faces coming in here."

"Doing well this season, Franco?" I said.

"In every sense of the word. Is that why you're here? To see how I've been?"

It wasn't, and we both knew it.

"Not really, Franco. What we're here for is some answers, and we need them now. What have you been up to with Benny Hinkle?"

"The fat little guy that runs the Sorbonne?" He scrunched his eyebrows. "Haven't seen him in a long time."

"Bullshit!" I snapped. "I know better and, as if you don't already know, he's dead."

At that, Franco did look surprised. Whether or not he was putting it on, I didn't know.

He frowned, jerked his head and said, "He's dead? What the hell happened?"

I gave him the short version. Of course, he denied any knowledge of what had happened to Benny, but he'd given up trying to act as if he hadn't seen Benny in a while. I figured Franco was smart enough to know that if we were there asking him questions, we had evidence to the contrary.

"So," I said. "Tell me about the poker games."

He stared at me for a moment, then looked at his two thugs, nodded, and they left... When I say they left, they moved away along the bar, just out of earshot, but close enough if they were needed in a hurry.

"So, you know about that, huh?" he said, his back still to the bar, his elbows on the bar top. "Hinkle wasn't just the owner of the Sorbonne. He was also... let's call him a professional snitch."

"A snitch?"

"He was in the business of buying and selling information; he was a broker. Hard for that man to keep his tongue from wagging, so after a couple—well, more than a couple— of faux pas, he decided to make a little money out of it."

Franco went around the bar, took two bottles of iced wine from a mini fridge and set them on the bar where a waitress was waiting to collect them. Then he came back, leaned in over the bar and, in a low voice said, "Those games were actually meetings. That was when we cashed in what we knew. We traded stories from all around the city. Stories about the little guys, stories about the powerful ones in expensive suits that are crushing them and much more. And Benny made money. He made others money too. A thousand, just for showing up."

"Really?" I said.

A smile spread across Franco's face and he nodded. "Oh, we played poker. We all enjoyed it. The money we played with wasn't usually our own... well, it was. Sometimes, sure, we brought it with us. But a lot of times, players got their stake from Benny in return for what they knew. Sometimes they'd walk away with an extra handful, sometimes with nothing. It was Benny's enterprise. And a damn good one, I'd say."

"You mean you just told him what you knew," I said, "in front of everyone else?"

"Nah! We handed it to him when we got there. In his office. Envelopes. That room, the game, it was Benny's way of providing us with anonymity, a cover. He was a smart little dude, in some ways."

Kate shook her head, shocked by what we were hearing. And I have to admit, so was I. I wouldn't have thought Benny was smart enough. The news was... stunning, and if he really was a snitch, it provided us with motive. But rather than providing us with any new leads, it opened up a whole new world of questions and, not only that, it made just about every ne'er do well in the city a suspect.

Franco's face? He was loving it. He knew just what it all meant, and he was playing it for all he was worth.

"What about you, Franco?" I asked. "Are you running an enterprise of your own?"

"Oh, come now, Harry," he said, spreading his arms and cocking his head to one side. "I'm clean. A reformed man. Nah! I hear things. So I made a few extra bucks. So what?"

He could have sworn up and down for a month of

Sundays that he was clean, but I'd never have believed him. The two thugs at the other end of the bar told a different story. They were obviously packing. When Franco saw me eyeing them, he laughed.

"Tony and Lou? They're here for my protection, Harry."

"Aren't they always?" I said dryly.

"I keep them around so my days running with the mob don't come back to haunt me," Franco replied. "I made more enemies than I did friends in that life. Nowadays, I just want to run this place in peace."

"Is that so?" Kate asked. She'd been so quiet I'd almost forgotten she was standing next to me.

"Business has been declining, believe it or not. It's just not what it used to be now that Sal is gone."

I was surprised by his somber tone. He looked out at the dining room as he spoke. It was indeed quieter than I remembered it. Especially around lunchtime. I had to admit it; back in the day it was something special. Some of Sal's touches still remained. They'd dug out the red bows and lights that he'd always hung up around the restaurant during the holidays.

"Well," Franco said after a moment. "I'm going to fix that. I want to start putting more time and money into the place. I'd hate to see what once was a great Italian restaurant here in Chattanooga shut down."

"That would be a shame," I admitted.

He stood there, leaning on the bar, waiting for us to walk away. We didn't budge.

He grinned and said, "I can tell you have more you want to ask me, Harry."

"Did you kill Benny?" I asked.

His eyes stayed locked on mine. The cockiness was

gone. Now he was serious.

"No."

How did I know he'd say that?

"D'you know who did?"

"No."

"No one at the game had a score to settle?" I persisted.

"People are always mad when they lose, Harry. You know that. Mad when they waste their money, but I wouldn't peg anyone at that table as a killer."

I looked again at his armed men, then back at him. He narrowed his eyes, locked them onto mine, pursed his lips and sucked the inside of his cheek.

"But what can I say?" he asked lightly. "People do crazy things when they're angry."

"That they do, Franco," I replied. "Besides Benny, you and Rod Harris, there were five other people at that poker table. Who are they?"

He grinned and said, "You know I can't tell you that, Harry. It would be more than my life's worth."

"Tell me about that night, Franco," I said.

"Which night?"

"Last Sunday, when Benny was killed."

He shrugged and more or less repeated the same story as Rod Harris had given us. He arrived a few minutes before nine, saw the commotion out back and left.

"So where were you between seven and nine?" Kate asked.

"That's easy, sweetheart. I was out and about running some errands, then I went to the Sorbonne to play poker."

"Anyone see you when you were *out and about*? And don't call me sweetheart."

He shrugged and said, "I'm sure there were plenty, but who they were, I have no idea."

"Where exactly did you go?"

"I went to Walmart for one," he replied and grinned. "Then I went to the Costco. That help?"

Son of a bitch, I thought. *He knows damn well we can't fact-check him there.*

"We need those names, Franco," I said.

He grinned and replied, "And I need to keep on breathing. I don't swim too well wearing concrete boots."

I thanked him for what little information he'd given us and we turned to leave. The smell of the cooking, however, was beginning to get to me, so I asked Kate if she wanted something to eat, and she didn't hesitate to pick a place just down the street.

"You know what?" Franco caught up with us just before we reached the door.

"What?" I asked.

"Merry Christmas, both of you."

I stopped, turned and looked at him. Franco de Luca, the "former" mob boss was holding out his hand for me to shake. He looked... as if he really meant it. So I took a step forward and shook his hand. His grip was firm, not what I'd expected. In the dim light of the restaurant, he still looked like the ghoul we'd seen on camera. His face had hardened over the years, if that was even possible. And he still had the air of a powerful man, a man you wouldn't want to be on the wrong side of.

But it was his eyes that really got my attention. They hadn't softened, not quite that. But now that I had a chance to really look at him in person, to see him again closeup, I couldn't deny there'd been a shift. He looked... lost.

"Merry Christmas, Franco."

Chapter Twenty-One

Wednesday Afternoon 1pm

Fifteen minutes later Kate and I were seated at a small Mexican restaurant. The food came quickly, and I was grateful for that. After all the coffee I'd consumed that day, on so little sleep, I was fighting a headache.

We gave ourselves a quiet moment before discussing what had just happened with Franco. When we did, I could tell she was as bothered as I was.

"So, we really think Benny Hinkle was running an operation like that?" she said before she spooned refried beans into her mouth. "I know what little evidence we have indicates that a lot of what Franco said is true. But do we really think Benny had the... the intelligence, the sophistication to pull something like this off?"

I had to hand it to her; Kate always did have a way of saying what I was thinking.

I thought for a moment, then shook my head and said,

"Nope. That's what's been bothering me, too. I just don't see it."

I devoured what was left of my taco before explaining my train of thought.

"Benny was obviously smarter about some things than I would ever have given him credit for. And it's clear to me now that the hidden cameras we found were his."

"Right," Kate said.

"The problem is, it's still too... technically sophisticated. He just wasn't that smart. I don't buy it. Was he capable of arranging secret poker games? Sure. But Benny barely knew how to turn on the lights, much less install those sophisticated cameras. I mean, seriously, the man didn't have a clue."

"That's what I was thinking," Kate said.

"So," I said. "How could a man like Benny install and run an encrypted security system that was almost too difficult even for Tim to hack?"

"He either had a partner or he paid someone to do it for him," she said.

"Right," I said. "So which was it, partner or hacker?"

We finished our lunch and ordered hot chocolate and, after just a few sips, I began to feel as if I was halfway human again. The brain fog lifted a little and my head cleared. I still needed a good night's sleep. But slowing down like that and listening to the rain tick-tacking on the window was helping me think.

"Do you think Trish might be involved?" Kate asked.

I sighed and shook my head. "No, I don't think so. Or, at least, I don't think she was the one with the computer skills. I still want to ask her some more questions, though. I want to make sure of what she knows, or doesn't know, about the poker players. Laura too. She said she didn't know about the poker games, but maybe, if we show her the screenshots, she might recognize some of them... Hell, even one would be a bonus."

"I'd hate to think Laura was involved in something dirty," Kate said and sipped her chocolate.

"I don't think she was lying," I said. "I don't think she has it in her, but she may be trying to protect Benny, or the Sorbonne itself. Something like that can blur the moral boundaries of any normally law-abiding person."

Kate put down her cup and said, "What about the players? Do you think one of them could be his partner? What about de Luca?"

"De Luca? I don't know. I wouldn't put it past him. The others? Not Harris. I'm sure of that. Shady's pal? No, I don't think so. He's muscle. But the woman... Now there's an enigma for you. Who the hell is she, I wonder? And then there's the cameras to consider. D'you really think they'd just sit there every week if they knew about them? No, it would be too risky."

"Good thinking," Kate replied. "If someone at that table helped set up the equipment, I doubt they'd have been involved in Benny's death."

"But," I countered, "if we can't find footage of his murder, maybe that's the reason. Whoever it was knew where the cameras were and how to deal with them."

"But would we have any footage at all then?" Kate asked. "Why didn't they just take the cameras?"

"One was smashed, Kate. The one we found on Benny's desk. The one in the backroom was still in situ. I'm betting whoever was in Benny's office when I showed up was looking for the cameras. He smashed the one with Benny's murder on it in case he got caught. I heard a thud that night, just before I was shot at."

"So you're saying that whoever it was that installed those cameras was Benny's partner and his killer."

I shook my head in frustration. "I don't know. It's a puzzlement. Either the person who killed him was also his partner, as you said, or, the person who shot Benny wasn't his partner at all, and found the camera after the fact. And the second option doesn't seem likely because we didn't find the cameras until after we found Benny's body. But we may also be looking at it from the wrong angle. Think about what Franco told us. Benny was selling information. Information that could cause harm to any number of people, bad and good. That would have made him an awful lot of enemies. We could be looking for someone outside the poker game. And if that's the case, we're in a world of shit."

"I don't even want to think about that," she replied. "I think we should concentrate on the players... At least until we can eliminate them all. And we need to track down who shot at you last night."

"Right. No word from Corbin, I suppose?"

"Not so far," she replied. "He would have called me if someone had turned up at one of the hospitals with a gunshot wound. And, so far as I know, no dead bodies have turned up either."

We sat there quietly for a moment, then I said, "You know what I think? I think Benny wasn't just a broker. I think he was into blackmail. I think he learned something about somebody and was making them pay to keep him quiet. I'll go even further. I think he was probably black-mailing more than one person, maybe even a whole lot of people. He was making one hell of a lot of money, that's for sure."

"That's quite a theory, Harry," she said. "You really think he was a professional blackmailer? That would provide a motive to kill him, but how would we even begin to track the killer down?"

"Hmm," I replied. "As you said, I think maybe we should eliminate the players first. There's no point in opening that Pandora's box unless we have to."

Kate's phone buzzed. She had a text from Laura. She was showing Trish around the bar and wanted to take her to see Benny's office.

I leaned back in my seat, finished the dregs of my hot chocolate and said, "Let's go then. We need to talk to them anyway. I'll check in with my team to see if they've managed to identify any more of the players."

And I did, and they hadn't, though Tim was able to send images of each of the players to my cell phone.

Chapter Twenty-Two

Wednesday Afternoon 2:10pm

I'd spent more time at the Sorbonne over the past several days than I had all year, and there I was again. It was just after two in the afternoon. A uniformed officer was posted out front. On one hand, he looked as tough as any cop you'll ever meet, standing with his arms folded across his chest, a gun on his hip, and a stern expression on his face. On the other hand, this particular guard's name was Moose: a tall, heavyset Canadian man with white hair and bushy sideburns, a friendlier version of Jeff Bridges if it wasn't for the weapon.

"Good afternoon, Moose," Kate said as she cleared our entrance to the building.

He gave her a courteous nod. "Good afternoon, ma'am. Kinda chilly, right?"

She obviously knew him quite well because, as she signed us both in, she asked him to keep an eye on Samson for her.

He grinned at her and said, "Is it okay if I get him out of the car?"

She frowned at him, looked up and down the street, then said, "Sure, but keep him on a tight leash—there's one on the back seat—and don't leave your post."

"Thanks," he replied. "You got it, ma'am. I always wanted to be a canine officer."

"Then you should apply. I'll put in a good word for you. We won't be long."

CSI was done with the bar and the dining area. But Benny's office and the secret room were still off-limits, and Laura wasn't happy about it. She was even more annoyed when Kate told her that co-owner or not, after what had happened during the night, the office and back room would have to be reprocessed.

Kate went back there to check out the investigation so far and to make a call to check in with Corbin.

Me? I sat Laura and Trish down at a table in the bar. My gut was telling me they weren't involved, but it wasn't infallible, and I needed to be sure.

I began by asking a couple of warm-up questions, then I hit them with what we'd learned from Franco about Benny's little side business.

"Laura, Trish," I began, "did either of you know that Benny had a side hustle? Did you know he was gathering and selling... sensitive information?"

Laura's mouth dropped open. She was almost speechless. "What? No!" she spluttered. "What d'you mean, 'sensitive information'?"

"He was," I said, in the words of Franco de Luca, "a professional snitch. My own theory is that he was also a blackmailer and that's why he was killed."

They both stared at me in horror.

"I don't believe it," Laura said. "He couldn't... He wouldn't... you can't think that, Harry. You knew him almost as well as I did. He didn't have it in him."

"You'd be surprised what you don't know about people," I said. "Benny was motivated by money. You know that. People confided in him. He was my go-to guy. When I needed information, the first name that came into my head was Benny Hinkle, and he always came through for me. It's not that big of a stretch for him to decide to cash in on his extracurricular activities."

Laura was beside herself, still trying to fight what we'd learned about the man she'd worked with for so many years. I couldn't help but feel sorry for her.

Trish didn't say anything; her expression remained blank.

"Trish?" I said. "What about you? Did you know what your father was doing?"

She shook her head and said, "No... I didn't."

I sighed and took out my phone.

As you know, Tim had sent pictures of the players, so I pulled them up and handed the phone to Laura.

"Do either of you recognize any of the people in these photos? Flip to the right."

Trish didn't even need to look. She hadn't spent any time at all in Chattanooga until Bill Perks had contacted her.

Laura, however, took her time looking through the pictures, frowning in concentration.

"I've seen him in the bar a couple of times," she said, turning the phone so I could see it. It was Franco de Luca. I made a note of it and nodded. She flipped to the next image.

"And him," she said, again showing me the image. It was Shady's henchman.

She flipped through the rest of the six images and said, "That's it. I don't know no more."

"You're sure?" I said, looking her in the eye.

"I said I don't know any of the others. Didn't you hear me?" Oh, she was hot. She could have bitten a sixpenny nail in two.

"Who are the two I picked out anyway?" she asked.

"The first one is Franco de Luca. The other one... I don't know yet."

I took my phone from her, pocketed it, and moved on.

"We also think Benny must have had a partner," I said. "Do either of you have any idea who that might be?"

"Yeah," Laura snapped. "I was his partner and I had nothing to do with this... this... crazy scheme. I think you've gone out of your mind, Harry. I really do."

"Trish?" I said.

"No!" she replied. "I don't believe it either."

I watched them both. Their body language didn't give me anything.

"When are we going to be able to get into his office?" Laura snapped.

I looked her in the eye. She looked away.

"Why is that so important, Laura?"

"We just got back from Bill Perks' office. He called us in for a private reading of his will."

Trish was choking down tears. She let Laura do the talking.

"Everything he'd said in his video we watched was true. He left both of us a good chunk of money." She looked around the dining area. She seemed... both sad and angry at the same time.

131

"We're going to use some of the money he left us to remodel the place," she continued. "Both of us."

"Really?"

Trish nodded. "I'm going to be here in Chattanooga for a while."

"Yeah. We want to make the Sorbonne a bit classier," Laura explained. "We want to take out that wall over there and repaint everything, update the booths and the tables and chairs, and we want new lights and a proper security system. We've got a lot of ideas."

"That sounds... wonderful," I said.

"Yeah," Trish said. "It's, like, the right thing to do. We need to get over this and freshening the place up will help us move on," and with that she burst into tears.

By now, Chattanooga was aware that Benny had been murdered, though specifics hadn't yet been disclosed to the public.

"I'm not really sure what my dad's tastes were," Trish said, drying her eyes, "but Laura said she'd help."

That hit me like a ton of bricks.

Remodeling the Sorbonne? Oh no!

I understood the sentiment and wished them luck, but I wasn't happy about the idea. The Sorbonne was something of a rat hole, but it was also a part of Chattanooga's character, frequented by almost everyone, rich and poor alike. Benny was its driving force; the engine that kept it running. Now he was to be stripped away from his bar?

I looked around shaking my head, thinking back over the years. They say things need a woman's touch, and most things do, but the Sorbonne? I had to wonder what would happen to his sports memorabilia and collectibles. How much of it would they keep? One thing I hoped they'd keep was his obnoxious neon sign near the front; if not, I'd buy it from them. But that, of course, would have to come later.

I worked my way through my checklist, but it was futile. Neither one of them had anything. Trish seemed particularly cagey, dodging my questions either by letting Laura answer or just telling me over and over again that she didn't know. Then again, maybe it was just me overthinking it. It was likely that she really didn't know anything. Hell, if Laura had been unaware of Benny's schemes, how could his distant daughter in Atlanta know anything?

But you know, I had no idea why, but there was something about her I was unable to read, so I had no alternative but to give it up and move on, for then anyway.

"I want to seal up that poker room," she said suddenly, nodding to both Laura and me in affirmation. "I think that's important. Either that or I want to open it up to expand the office. But... I don't want any reminders that will..." She cleared her throat, "dredge up the memory of what happened to him. So it's probably better that we just seal it up and forget about it."

That, I could sympathize with. I looked at Laura, who shot me a pitiful look, then said, "Is there anything else you need from us, Harry?"

"No, I don't think so. Not for now, anyway."

I couldn't get over the fact that the two people closest to Benny didn't have a clue who he really was. Sure, he must have trusted them in some respects, but not with what really mattered. The man I thought I knew had turned into an enigma. As to Laura and Trish? I was digging a dry well.

When I asked Trish about her inheritance, she acted cagey, as if she was holding something back. Maybe she thought it was none of my business, and maybe she was right. But, even taking into account her secretiveness, I didn't think Trish was her father's partner in crime, if that's what his business was, which I sincerely hoped it wasn't.

And as for Laura, apart from the Sorbonne, I was now certain that she wasn't affiliated with any of Benny's money-making schemes.

Chapter Twenty-Three

Wednesday Evening 6:30pm

B y six that afternoon I was back in my office, signing off on several closed cases and clearing away some old papers and files before the New Year was upon us. I was hoping to be out of there by six-thirty so I could go home and get some rest. My entire body was beginning to ache. I was just about exhausted. And then, as it always happens, there was a knock at the door.

"Harry," Heather said as she stuck her head in. "We've got a solid list of names and contact info. You got a minute?"

Inwardly, I sighed. I *really* wanted to go home, but I didn't let them see it.

"Of course," I replied. "Come on in."

She stepped inside, followed by Tim. He presented me with a sheet of paper.

Between them, they'd managed to collect information on most of our suspects. Tim walked me through the first person they managed to track down.

"So, you were right that this guy is one of Shady's men.

His name is Jermaine King. He was evicted from his last known address, but we do know that he works at a strip club just outside of town."

"He's actually the owner," Heather interjected.

Wow.

"He does have a minor criminal record," Tim said, flipping to another document. "He had been in a couple of bar fights when he was younger, and he had another incident that was expunged. Overall, he seems to have a bit of a temper."

"We also found a couple of emails between him and Benny," Heather said. "But, there wasn't really anything in these exchanges that was incriminating."

Okay. It wasn't much, but it was still more than I'd expected. The Latino man with a goatee was Diego Trejo. Married with three kids, he was a carpenter who worked at a furniture restoration shop. They hadn't managed to find anything hinting at the illegal activity at the Sorbonne, but he had been arrested for assault a few years back, though the charges were dropped. I wasn't ready to rule out his involvement in Benny's death.

"What have you got on the others?" I asked.

They'd gathered locations and snippets of conversations for Franco de Luca and Rod Harris, but there wasn't anything more than Kate and I had learned that day.

Despite this, I was impressed.

"Nice work, guys. Truly. What about the last two?"

Tim sighed, clipped the papers together, and placed the packet on my desk.

"Well, that's where we've hit a wall. The younger guy and the woman have been a lot harder to track down. As far as I can tell, neither of them have records. We've combed through social media sites, but that's been a lot to navigate."

I sighed. You can't win them all.

"You've done great so far. Just keep working at it."

Tim looked at me, then lowered his eyes and said, "I'm thinking facial recognition."

I looked sharply at him. "Do we have that?" I asked, my eyes narrowed, knowing damn well we didn't.

"No, but the FBI does."

"No!" I snapped. "No... you... don't. You get caught hacking them and they'll be down here so fast it will take your breath away. Then they'll haul our asses off to jail. You are *not* to fool around with them. You understand, Tim?"

He nodded, grinned at me and said, "It was just a thought, Harry."

"Yeah, well," I said. "Stop thinking and go back to digging. Heather, you dig into Jermaine and Diego. I don't want to tip them off, so don't talk to them directly. We'll watch them from afar for now. So just ask around. Okay?"

"Yes, sir," she replied.

"And don't call me sir."

"No, sir," she replied smiling.

"Go on, get out of here, both of you. You did good. Now go home and get some rest."

We'd already talked to two of the people at the table and I wasn't about to trust Franco and Harris to keep their mouths shut forever. Especially when their poker games were based on swapping gossip from around town!

They bid me a good night and left, leaving me alone with the list. It'd been a long day for all of us and I was more than ready to go home. But I didn't. I moped around the office, did more paperwork, eager to get it cleared away and off my mind. I made myself a cup of coffee and took it back to my office and sat for a while by the great window, drinking it and watching the lights twinkling on the river.

Eight-thirty arrived and I was still there, alone in the office. All the lights were off except for mine and those in the lobby. It was time for me to leave, and I did. I called Amanda and told her I was on my way.

The drive home was uneventful. The roads were clear of ice and, for the most part, traffic. So it was no wonder, then, that my thoughts returned to the events of the day.

I was on MLK and about to go right onto Broad when I began to think about my conversation with Rod Harris.

I couldn't imagine him hooking up those two high-end spy cameras. He'd been a fair enough police officer; smart, intelligent, but I knew he wasn't tech savvy. And now he was out on parole, and that being so I found it hard to believe that he could have been heavily involved or invested in Benny's "professional snitching." He had too much to lose. So no, Rod Harris wasn't a likely suspect.

As much as I loathed what he'd done in the past, I had the feeling he really was determined to kick start his father's business into life again. Sincerity is hard to fake for most people, and even harder to maintain, and Rod wasn't exactly the master manipulator.

What about Franco? I thought.

A former mobster, a made man, trying to revitalize the local restaurant he'd inherited from his mob-connected older brother. A man standing behind a bar with two body-guards ready to protect him by any means necessary. His story that they were there solely for his protection seemed a little over the top, hard to believe. Men like those... they could be intimidating to anyone threatening you, that's for sure. But they'd also come in mighty handy if you wanted to intimidate someone on your to-do list.

I took the slipway off Highway 41 onto Scenic Highway and began the climb up the mountain. I was still physically tired, but my mind was working overtime, and I had a bad feeling in the pit of my gut that something was about to break.

I pulled off the road onto Cravens Terrace, close to the scene where Amanda had been driven off the road by Duvon James—another of Shady Tree's henchmen—took out my phone and called Kate.

"How tired are you, Kate?" I asked when she answered.

"I could stand another cup of coffee. What are you thinking?"

"How'd you like to come with me on a good ol' fashioned stake out?"

"Err... Okay... Who's our target?"

"Franco. Franco de Luca."

Chapter Twenty-Four

Wednesday Evening 9pm

I called Amanda and told her something had come up and that I might be late so not to wait up for me. Then I drove to Kate's apartment to pick her up.

She was wearing sweats and had her hair tied up in a bun on top of her head. As always, even in sweats, she looked... beautiful.

"Hey, here you go," she said and handed me my trusty CZ75. "Coffee first, then stakeout."

"Where's the pup?" I asked.

"He's staking out the couch," she replied with a grin.

"You leave him there by himself?"

"Sure. He's a good dog. Right now he's full of steak and kibbles and snoozing. He'll be fine."

I nodded and headed for Starbucks. Truth be told, I felt better now that I had my pal back. You never want things to escalate when you're on a stakeout, and it didn't happen often. But after seeing Franco's men earlier that day, it was reassuring to know that both Kate and I were armed.

We parked across the street from Franco's Italian restaurant, watching it like a pair of hawks. By then it was almost ten o'clock and the last customers were leaving. Franco was still in there. At least as far as we knew he was, so we had nothing to do other than wait and watch. Thus the conversation inevitably turned to? You guessed it: the festive season about to fall upon us.

"Any luck finding a Christmas present for Amanda?" she asked.

I laughed. "It's only been a few hours."

"You're running out of time, buddy."

"Huh, tell me about it," I replied. "You know, I had this funny feeling when we were talking to Harris this afternoon."

"You mean you think he was lying? I know what you mean, because some of what he said is bothering me, too."

"Hmm. Lying isn't the exact word I'd use," I said. "Unless we're talking about lying by omission. I think most of what he told us was probably true, but I do think he was holding back. And there were several times when he just wouldn't make eye contact with me. I have the feeling there's a storm brewing, Kate, that something's about to break. We've already uncovered more than I ever thought we would. But still, it's eating away at me, this feeling that the other shoe hasn't yet dropped."

"I didn't tell you, Harry, but when I got back to the PD I did call Harris's parole officer," Kate said, deep in thought.

"And?" I rolled my shoulders, yawned and turned my head from side to side in an effort to ease the tightness in my neck.

"They've been keeping an eye on him, obviously. His parole officer knew about his visits to the Sorbonne, but as far as he knew, Harris was just going there for drinks. I didn't mention the gambling... He told me he'd heard a rumor that he may be stealing cars, but they don't have any proof. Geez, Harry, if it comes out that he was consorting with known felons and I didn't report it, my ass will be in a sling."

"Your call, Kate," I replied. "You know whatever you decide, I'll back you. What about the stolen cars? You think there's anything to it?"

"I'm not sure, but so far Harris has managed to keep his nose clean and stay out of trouble; that, according to his parole officer. I don't think he had anything to do with Benny's murder, and he sure couldn't have installed those two cameras. He doesn't have the skills. Yes, he probably does need the extra cash; I'll give him that. As to car theft? Who cares? That's for someone else to figure out, right?"

"I agree," I said. "He didn't do it, but he might know who did. I think he knows more than he's telling. Maybe we should talk to him again."

"Yes," she replied. "He sure as hell rubs me the wrong way. I can't stand crooked cops. Still, after all this time... I guess he paid for his sins."

I could have said the same about de Luca. Why else would we have been camped out in front of his business? The guy was a creep. He was dirty. He was as crooked as a bent corkscrew, and we all knew it. And I knew deep in my gut that he had to be involved in something nefarious. Just what, I had no idea.

Eventually the conversation turned to the other players.

"You know, I don't think it's a coincidence that four out of the six have criminal records," I said. "We know de Luca, Harris and King do. The other guy... What was his name, Trejo? Apart from an assault charge, he's clean. The other two? I guess we'll know soon enough. What did Tim call them? The Legion of Doom? He may be right. These people could be running the city from the shadows!"

Kate laughed. "That's ridiculous, Harry. You're becoming paranoid in your old age."

"Old age? What the hell are you talking about, Kate? I'm only forty-six; not much older than you, damn it."

"Hey, take it easy, buddy. I was just pulling your chain."

"I know," I said. "I'm sorry. I'm just irritable. Comes from lack of sleep, I guess."

"That's better," she replied. "Look, if these poker players were involved in exchanging information for money, they had to be getting their knowledge from somewhere, right? Maybe we should just go on in there and apply a little pressure. Often the best way to obtain that kind of information is to be involved in it yourself."

I didn't really hear that last part. I was still thinking about her earlier comment.

Paranoid? Is she serious?

Maybe she *was* right. Maybe I was being paranoid. If I was, I had every right to be. Look who we were dealing with. I don't care how sincere Franco's little song and dance about being a changed man was. There was a time when he'd threatened everyone close to me, and that was something I would never forget.

"He's like frickin' Shady Tree," I said aloud.

"What?"

"Franco. He's like Shady Tree."

The only other person I'd ever encountered during my time as a cop and a PI who threatened my life, and the lives of my loved ones, was Shady. And boy, oh boy, did he ever follow through on his promises. Amanda, after being run off the road on the mountain by one of his henchmen, had finished physical therapy only a few months ago. He'd bombed my old offices, and he'd framed me for the murder of a Texas ranger. He managed to pull that off from the grave. He put me and my family through hell... and I got mad every time I thought about it. *Son of a bitch. May he rot in hell. Yes, I'm paranoid. Who wouldn't be?*

"Harry..." Kate said and put her hand on my arm. Obviously, she could see my blood was about to runneth over.

It was difficult to ignore! Shady had, in some ways, ruined my life. He'd almost managed to kill me in Mexico. Anyone setting off alarm bells the way he did was bound to make me testy. Franco de Luca was one of them.

But Kate was right. I needed to get over it. I was working. I needed to focus. So I nodded, said nothing and continued to watch the restaurant. She took her hand off my arm and we sat there in silence until, some fifteen minutes or so later, we spotted a shadowy figure walking toward us on the opposite side of the street.

He stopped in front of the building and stood there for a moment staring at the front entrance. I squinted. I could tell it was a man, but it was too dark to recognize him. I knew it wasn't Franco. Nor was it either of his two soldiers.

"Can you see who it is?" I asked.

Kate slowly shook her head as we watched the guy pull the front door open. She opened her mouth to answer, then sat up straight and said, "Oh, my God. He's got a gun."

"Holy..." I began as I jerked on the door handle, shoved the door open, and almost fell in my rush to get out of the car.

We both drew our weapons and, as we ran across the street, we heard a series of gunshots ring out from inside the restaurant.

We hit the two steps running, then onto the porch. I jerked the door open. We paused.

"*Police!*" Kate shouted. "Drop your weapons." She pushed me to one side, twisted her body to the left around the door frame and ducked inside, her Glock in both hands.

That was frickin' reckless, I thought as I followed her in, twisting to the right.

Chapter Twenty-Five

Wednesday Evening 10:30pm

The interior of the restaurant was dim, almost dark. Half the lights had been turned off. Kate crouched behind the hostess stand near the front, where I heard her whispering into her phone. Me? I carefully crept to a half wall and took cover behind it; not that it would have provided much protection. It was just studs and wood paneling.

I cautiously peered around, scanning the dining area. There wasn't much to see. One, it was dark, and two, there were no people; at least none that I could see. Not then.

"Hey, Franco," I shouted.

"Harry?" the voice came from somewhere at the far end of the room.

"Franco. It's me and Captain Gazzara. We're coming to you. If you and your goons are carrying, put your weapons down on the floor."

The rest of the lights went on, flooding the restaurant with a soft amber glow.

I stood up. So did Kate.

Franco was maybe five feet in front of the bar, crouching beside and staring at a body on the floor. He rose to his feet as we approached, our weapons in both hands.

"He's dead," Franco told Kate.

"I figured as much," she said. "I already called it in."

"Tony." He nodded in the direction of the wall at the far end of the bar. "He got hit.

Tony had indeed got hit, in the shoulder. He was on his backside propped up against the wall, blood oozing from the wound. The other thug, Lou was applying pressure. Tony's face was twisted in pain and his right leg was jerking uncontrollably.

"What the hell happened, Franco?" I asked. "You need to put that down now." He was still holding the gun at his side.

Franco ignored me. His face was set, his eyes cold.

"The bastard came in and tried to blow our heads off. Tony there was hit trying to protect me. I managed to fire a round and killed him, the crazy son of a bitch."

Franco turned a little to his left, looked at Tony and shook his head.

"It was self-defense," he snarled. "They were both doing their jobs."

"Franco," Kate snapped, her weapon pointed directly at him. "Do as Harry said and put... the gun... down. Do it now."

He glared at her, the gun still at his side, but he was standing with his feet apart as if he was an old west gunslinger daring us to make a move. If someone was to ask me to describe Franco de Luca, that was the image that would come to mind.

"Franco," I said gently, putting my own firearm away.

"We got this, so do as she says and give her your weapon before you get hurt. We know what happened. We saw the guy outside with a gun. You have a solid self-defense plea, so don't screw it up. Give her the gun."

He stood for a moment, not saying a word, then nodded, reversed the weapon, held it by the barrel and handed it to her.

The door opened and a half-dozen officers rushed in, weapons drawn.

The guy in the lead, a sergeant, spotted Kate immediately. He obviously knew her because he held up his hand for the rest of his team to stop where they were.

"What ya got, Captain?" the sergeant asked, his gun still in his hand. "We got a 'shots fired' call."

Kate explained what had happened, and the sergeant—she called him Jim—had his guys collect the four weapons, including the victim's. No one protested. Tony's face was a sickly white. One of Jim's officers told him an ambulance was on the way. I'm not sure if Tony heard. His eyes were closed and his chin was on his chest.

While it would have been simple just to take Franco's word for it, there was no way to verify exactly what had happened. Yes, we saw an armed man run into the restaurant and we heard gunshots, but how it went down... there was no way to tell. Kate, however, had no alternative but to take his word for what had happened, especially knowing that both of his goons would back up his story.

Me? I didn't know; still don't. Knowing Franco as I did, however, I had a feeling there was more to it. Yes, the guy went in there with a gun. Did Franco or one of his goons fear for their lives? I'm sure they did. And in Tennessee that makes it a clear case of self-defense.

And then something strange happened. As if on cue, in walked Benny's lawyer Bill Perks.

"Bill," I said as he walked up to Franco and shook his hand. "What the hell are you doing here?"

"I represent Mr. de Luca," he replied. "I got a call and came over as soon as I heard what happened."

"You what?" Kate said. She was as stunned as I was.

I stared at Perks in disbelief. He really did look like Benny. Now more than ever. He was even sweating like him. It was freezing cold outside, and this man was sweating buckets.

"Franco, you need to tell us what happened," I said.

Perks immediately opened his mouth to protest. I cut him off.

"Franco, listen to me," I said. "Mine and Kate's testimony is what's going to keep you out of jail. So let's have it. Tell us exactly what happened here."

He was quiet for a moment. I couldn't tell if he was going to talk or take a swing at me.

"Fine," he replied. "It happened just like I said. He came in here and started shooting. He took us by surprise. He got Tony with his first shot. I grabbed my Glock and I shot him. That's it."

"Why did he want to kill you?" Kate asked.

He shrugged, then said, "You need to take a look at a guy named Porter. He was one of the players at the poker games. He's one shifty son of a bitch. Go talk to him."

"Porter?" I asked. "He's responsible for this? He's the young guy, right?"

Before he could give me an answer, Perks jumped in and shut it down.

"That's enough, Franco," he said. "Don't say another word, you hear?"

He turned to Kate and said, "Are you going to arrest my client? Yes or no?"

Kate glanced at me, then back at Perks and said, "No. Not at this time. But he is going to have to make a formal statement. After that... well, that's for others to decide." Then she turned and said, "Sergeant. Take Mr. de Luca to the police department and take his statement. Mr. Perks, you're welcome to join them at the PD. Right now, we need to clear the restaurant. CSI will be here shortly to process the place."

Jim, the sergeant, grabbed Franco's arm and led him, without protest, out to his cruiser, passing the paramedics on the way.

Bill Perks remained, standing next to Kate, who pointedly ignored him. The last I saw of him, he was slinking down the aisle and out of the building.

"Harry," Kate said. "Come here. Take a look at who it is."

I'd been so caught up in the chaos and mayhem with the sleazy mobster and his lawyer, I hadn't had a chance to really look at the body. He was lying on his back, one leg folded beneath him, his arms spread, his face staring up at the ceiling. I bent down to get a better look.

"Geez, that's... Kate, that's the Latino from the poker games. Diego Trejo."

Chapter Twenty-Six

Thursday Morning 9:40am

After returning home at a little after midnight from the second gunfight I'd been involved in in less than twenty-four hours, I went straight to bed and crashed, ever grateful that my long-suffering wife Amanda understood.

The next morning I was up and awake with the birds at around five-thirty. I figured that it was going to be a busy day and that I didn't have time for my usual six-mile run so I decided to do some laps. It had been a week or two since I'd done that, and even though the water was heated to a balmy seventy-two degrees, the open air was not. Up there on the mountain top that morning it was a crisp thirty degrees. Now, with the wind blowing in off the valley, that's mighty cold, I can tell you.

I did thirty laps, climbed out of the pool, and the wind hit me. I quickly grabbed my beach towel, wrapped it around me and ran into the house to find Amanda in the kitchen laughing at me. It was just after six and Jade and Maria were still in bed.

"I bet that washed the cobwebs out of your system," she said as she watched me stand there shivering as I sipped the first cup of coffee of the day. "Why were you so late again last night? What happened?"

I gave her the short version, trying to downplay what could have been a dangerous situation.

Amanda, having been a popular news anchor for Channel 7 TV, knew Franco personally and she'd never liked him.

"Are they going to charge him?" she asked.

I shook my head and told her I doubted it, that it seemed to be a clear-cut case of self-defense.

"Really?" she asked skeptically.

She cooked me some scrambled eggs, which I ate with relish along with a second cup of coffee, and then I dressed, looked in on the still sleeping Jade, told Amanda I'd call her later to let her know what was going on, then I drove to the office, hoping to get there before anyone else.

Of course, I didn't. I sometimes think Jacque is blessed with ESP because, no matter what time I arrive, she always seems to get there before me, and that Thursday was no exception. I found her in the breakroom where I joined her for my third cup of coffee of the morning. By the time I'd finished that one, I was beginning to feel the jolt from the excess of caffeine.

By eight-forty-five I was waiting for Heather to arrive. She was due in at nine. I ambushed her in the lobby, coffee in one hand, breakfast sandwich in the other.

"No time to go to your desk, Heather," I said, taking her by the arm and turning her around. "You can eat that in the car. We're going to interview Jermaine King at his club."

Heather Stillwell is the poster girl for good health. I say girl; she's actually forty years old but doesn't look a day older than thirty. She's five-eight with short brown hair, an oval face, brown eyes, and a slim, hard body. She works out for an hour every morning, teaches self-defense in her spare time, and is an expert shot. She spent the first two years of her law enforcement career as a street cop in Atlanta, where she caught the eye of a hotshot from the GBI—the Georgia Bureau of Investigation—who recruited her. She was immediately fast-tracked for high office, but something went wrong. What it was, to this day I still don't know. She never would talk about it. I'd met her on several occasions during the course of one investigation or another, and I was impressed.

Then, one day I got a call from her. She wanted to know if I had any openings. It just so happened that I did, and I hired her over the phone. I did ask her why she left the GBI, but she said she'd rather not talk about it, and I respected that. I had my suspicions that it was because of a personal relationship. You see, Heather's gay, and she's proud of it. She's been a great addition to my team. Since Bob Ryan left, she's taken over as my head field investigator.

Anyway, that morning... I don't know if it was because she was with me, or maybe it was just because it was so early, but for whatever reason, Heather was decidedly uncomfortable when we stepped out of the watery sunlight into the dimly lit Passions, the quintessential "titty bar."

It wasn't quite ten o'clock, but there were already dancers on stage. What was even crazier to see was the small cluster of customers, some drinking beer, some drinking hard liquor. And I had to wonder at the makeup of such people, people who were willing to watch nude women dance, no matter the time of day. Even for frickin' breakfast.

We stepped up to the bar and I asked the scantily clad young woman bartender where Jermaine was, and she went to fetch him.

Much like Rod Harris, when he slunk out of the shadows and saw me waiting for him his eyes grew wide, then he tried to play it as if he wasn't surprised to see me. Unfortunately for him, it didn't work.

"Harry Starke," he said from behind the bar. "What you doin' here?"

"Ah-ha," I said when I got a good look at his face. "Now I remember you."

"You... what?" he asked.

I really did remember him and I couldn't help but smile. "Didn't I break your nose back in the day?"

Heather slipped her hand under her jacket. I put my hand on her arm. She relaxed.

I wasn't there to start a fight, and judging by Jermaine's demeanor, he wasn't about to start swinging either.

"Look," he sputtered. "I don't want no trouble. No trouble, okay? I swear, I'm clean. Ask anybody and they'll tell ya." His words were coated with a thick, southern drawl. I hate to stereotype the accent, I really do, but my memories of the altercations I'd had with him and his old boss, Shady Tree, painted him as something of a simpleton.

"What are you doing here?" I asked. "I figured you'd be in prison."

"Hah, so you say," he said. "Shady done took care of me. He always did. He gave me enough to buy this place. It be the only twenty-four-hour titty bar in Chattanooga." He actually sounded proud.

When he saw Heather's grimace, he scoffed. "Make that face all ya want, sister. This be a good business."

"Easy," I said. "You said you don't want trouble. Don't disrespect my associate."

He looked... a little deflated.

"So how come you're not in prison, Jermaine?" I asked. "I was sure you would be."

Aside from the record Tim and Heather had unearthed, I'd personally made sure several of Shady's men went away after what they'd done to me, my team, and my family.

"I was! I got six months for possession of a stolen gun on'y I din't steal it. I did what I was supposed to in there. An', I never shot nobody. I on'y ever intimidated people, like Shady ast me to, y'know?"

"Oh, I do know," I replied. And I did. That was how Shady worked. He was always more bark than bite. But when it was time for someone to get bitten, he made sure it would hurt.

"I hear you've been playing poker with Benny Hinkle and some other folks," I said.

"What? He looked gobsmacked. "How d'you know that?"

"Let's just say I know and get on with it," I said. "I also know you were exchanging information for cash."

"Uh-uh," he said, shaking his head violently.

"Come on, Jermaine," I said. "We know all about it. The poker game was just a front. You, and the other players, met each week to cash in your information with Benny."

"How d'you know that?" he repeated.

"Did you know he was murdered last Sunday night?"

"Uh-uh. I din't know that." He shook his head again.

"Where were you last Sunday night between seven and eight?"

"Me?" he asked.

"Yes, you. Who the hell did you think I was talking to, Jermaine? Where were you?"

"Between sev'n an' eight? I was here. Ask anybody."

"What about the game Sunday night?" I asked.

"What about it?"

"Geez, Jermaine," I replied. "It's like talking to a knot on a log, talking to you. Did you go to the poker game on Sunday night?"

"No. It was canceled."

"How did you know?"

"'Cause there was a bunch of police cars an' stuff out back, is how I know."

"So you did go to the game?"

"No. It was canceled, like I told ya. You not hearing right or somethin'?"

I shook my head in frustration.

"Okay, okay," I said. "So you went to the game and you figured it was canceled because of the police cars, is that right?"

"Y...eah."

"What time did you get there?" I asked.

"I dunno... sometime around nine, I guess, maybe a little earlier. I wasn't payin' no attention was I?"

I sighed and said, "Okay. So we've established the fact that you were a regular player, now tell how it worked. What kind of information were you selling to Benny?"

"Um... er..." He looked sheepishly at me, shook his head, and sighed. "All sorts o' stuff. Lots of business guys come in here. They drink. They get lit. They say all sorts of stuff they shouldn't, 'specially to the girls. Benny had the same setup over at his bar. When people got alcohol in 'em, they kinda don't give a shit about what they sayin', you know? Their tongues get real loose. Benny, he paid good money for it."

"One of the players was a young guy," I said.

"Yeah. So what?"

"What's his name?" I asked.

"Ah... no, no, no. I ain't getting into none o' that. You think I wanna get my ass killed? You crazy, man."

Geez, how did I know that?

"And the woman?" I said, not expecting an answer. I wasn't disappointed.

"Uh-uh. No way."

I asked him several more questions but received only similar answers, so I gave it up. It was no surprise that Jermaine King was a dead end. He was dead from the neck up!

Chapter Twenty-Seven

Thursday Morning 10:45am

I wanted to keep up the momentum I had going, but I had no one else to interview. The only other player we'd been able to identify so far was Diego Trejo, and he was dead. Shot to death by Franco de Luca.

What the hell was his beef with Franco? I wondered as we walked out of Passions into the sunlight. *I guess we may never know. And this Porter guy Franco mentioned. Who's he? And the woman...*

I called Kate.

"Harry. I can't talk now. I'm in a meeting and I'm going to be tied up with more meetings all morning. Being a captain's a real bitch sometimes."

"I was hoping you'd come with me to talk to Diego's family," I said.

"Can't, not until this afternoon. Sorry. Gotta go. Talk later when I get through."

"Well, there's no way I'm going alone, so let's get together this afternoon."

"I'll call you later. Bye." And with that, she hung up.

Me? I thought for a minute, halfway decided to take Heather, then decided there was something else I really needed to do, something I'd been putting off for almost a month, so I decided against it and we went back to the office.

"Harry," she said as we pulled into the parking lot.

"Yes?"

"I wanted to say how sorry I am about Benny." She smiled and put her hand on my shoulder. "I know it's already been almost a week, and I know you're working tirelessly through this all. But, if there's anything more I can do, you only have to ask."

"Thank you, Heather," I said, and I meant it.

I checked in with Jacque, then went to my office and logged into my computer and started looking around at the local spas. Kate was right. A day at the spa would be a great Christmas gift for Amanda. Knowing her, though, I figured she'd want to do something together and I wasn't sure how I felt about that. Not that I'd complain about a massage. With the way the weather was, and with everything that was going on, I hadn't been running or swimming as much as I would have liked, and I was feeling it in my muscles, especially in my back. Loosening them up would do me some good.

But couples massages... that just seemed weird to me, so I set that idea aside for the moment.

I was browsing the online jewelry stores as a backup when there was a knock on the door and Tim stuck his head inside.

"Morning, Harry. Got something for you." He handed me a thumb drive. "I managed to recover the footage of all the poker games the camera recorded over the last two months."

"Two months?" I said. "Tim, that's great. Well done."

"Thanks. You're welcome." He shoved his glasses further up the bridge of his nose and squinted at me. "See, with how much money Benny had in his safe, and in his bank accounts, and the timeline of things with Trish and all, I was pretty sure there must have been plenty of other poker games before the first one you have on that drive. I don't think the camera was set up until two months ago."

"Maybe something triggered Benny into taking extra precautions," I said. "Maybe he was becoming paranoid and was trying to protect himself. Who knows?"

Tim poked his glasses again and nodded. "I decrypted them all, but none of them have audio. I don't think the cameras were ever set to record sound. Only video."

"That's odd..." I said, frowning.

"Why's that?"

"Well, you'd think Benny would have wanted to record the sound... I just don't get it. Benny was trading information, and he was in deep. The players were trading secrets. Benny was buying them. Everyone was lining their pockets with money. The people around that table were dirty, so we have to assume that he'd want to record what they were saying. The recordings were his insurance policy. There was also the opportunity for blackmail. Now I'm not saying that's what he was into, but we have to take it into consideration."

"You really think he had that in him?" Tim asked. "Blackmail? That's really serious stuff, Harry."

"It's a possibility," I replied. "Money talks. Big money corrupts... Kate and I, we think he had a partner, Tim. A

160

ghost. His business was secrets. Secrets are valuable to the right buyer. So why not record the audio? It makes no sense."

Tim just shook his head. "I can't imagine how exhausting it must have been for him, living a double life and having to keep tabs on so many people."

"Well," I replied, "from what I'm hearing, it wasn't just the poker players he had to keep tabs on. He had dirt on some pretty dangerous people."

I brought Tim up to speed on what had happened at Franco's restaurant the night before.

"...and I'm not sure Franko didn't murder Trejo," I said, thinking out loud. "Sure, Trejo had a gun, but did he intend to use it? Did he take it there for self-defense? I just don't know, and I sure as hell don't trust Franco. One thing he did do, though, was give us a name: Porter. I think it's the young man, the player we've yet to identify. See what you can find. If it's him... We need a break, Tim. We also need to know who the woman is. I have a feeling about her. Hell, Porter could be a first name or a surname, in which case it could be the woman. We need to know one way or the other, so that's your priority."

I had a hunch that every last one of those six poker players was a crook, and I was being proved right time and time again!

"Look out of state, too, Tim. If it comes to it... that facial recognition thing."

"But—"

"Don't ask, Tim. You know what my answer will be."

"On it, boss. I think you'll want to watch the footage, though. The guy—I'll call him Porter for now. He's the big loser. He always lost money. He'd bet the highest, too. He'd bring in a lot of his own cash and almost always lose it all by the end of the night. Sometimes it was several hundred. Other times, he lost several thousands of dollars."

"He doesn't sound like much of a poker player, then," I said.

"I watched them all, Harry. It was every game. I just don't know how you go to that many games and lose that badly. Where did he get that kind of money anyway? We need to study the tapes. There's something fishy about it."

I agreed. In a game that involved a fair bit of luck and a whole lot of skill, it sounded to me as if Porter was dumping money.

"Do you think his money was counterfeit?" Tim asked. "And he was trying to get rid of it?"

"It's possible, I suppose... Okay, go on. Get back to work while I go through the footage. Find me some names."

And he left, and I didn't... watch the footage, that is. I needed to find a gift for Amanda and I was running out of time. It was my own damn fault. I would have asked Jacque or Kate to find something, but that would be... not the right thing to do. I'd procrastinated for so long, and I was trying to persuade myself that it was because I didn't want to get her the wrong thing. It was the same every year. I put it off and put it off until... well, you get the idea. And now there I was trying to decide which stone would look best around Amanda's neck.

When twelve o'clock rolled around, I texted her and told her I'd meet her at the country club as an apology for working so late the past few nights. *Yeah*, I thought, *a nice lunch.*

But it wasn't just that. I needed a break. And the club was beautiful at Christmastime.

I'd been a bear since Benny died, and I needed to make up for it. I also needed to spend a little quality time with Amanda, and I was looking forward to it.

Chapter Twenty-Eight

Thursday Midday

The Country Club was, as I expected, decked out for the holidays with immaculately decorated trees, garlands, and a myriad of classic Christmas decorations: Lots of glass and snowflake ornaments and colored lights hung from the ceiling. Despite a near-perfect balance of tasteful and kitschy, however, there were a number of gaudy pieces that made my skin crawl. There was, for instance, a small, dusty pink tree near the bar that looked downright tacky. But even that one had Amanda beaming.

"Oh, come on, Harry," she said. "It's so over the top it's cute."

Me? Hah, no ma'am.

In truth, anytime I saw something like that tree, I understood how Charlie Brown felt when he was disappointed by all the commercialization.

Amanda was wearing a white sweater and a black skirt. Her hair, now grown out, was swept back in a ponytail. She looked... stunning, and I had to wonder how I managed to get so lucky.

She'd arrived a little after noon and joined me at the bar. I ordered dry white wine for her; I already had my Laphroaig. They keep a bottle behind the bar especially for me.

We sat together at my favorite table in the great bay window overlooking the ninth green. Amanda ordered a Greek salad and I ordered some stuffed mushrooms.

"So," Amanda said, "what's going on? I've barely seen you these last few days. Fill me in. Is everything okay? What's going on with your Benny investigation?" she asked as she dug into her salad.

"Wow," I said. "All those questions." I guess it was the reporter in her.

I looked at her, thinking how lucky she was to still be alive.

She was an anchor for Channel 7 TV when I first met her. She didn't like me then, and I sure as hell didn't like her. A year earlier she'd done an on-air profile of me... When I say profile, I mean it was a hatchet job, and I swore she'd never get the chance to do it again. Funny how times and situations change.

She wore her blonde hair bobbed back then, cut three inches below the point of her chin. She looked like a pixie with pale green eyes. She walked into my office one day and demanded an interview, and... well, things progressed from there. Now, here she was, the love of my life.

"It's... kind of complicated," I said and locked eyes with her. I'd already told her the short version of what had happened at the Sorbonne when I'd walked in on the intruder, and what had happened at Franco's restaurant, but not in any great detail.

Amanda never pressed me to talk about my work, or my cases, but she knew me well enough to know when I needed to discuss what was going on. She's analytical and attentive to detail and can often spot nuances I miss. She's also a great sounding board. So, as we ate, I unloaded, not really talking to her but basically thinking out loud.

She ate in silence as I droned on and on, quietly munching her lunch.

When I finished rattling on and I'd laid out all the details, she began to walk through it with me.

"So, you think more than one person orchestrated all of this?" she asked.

"I do," I replied. "I just can't see any of these people being involved with each other, or with Benny; there has to be someone else in the background. The only link we have between any of them, other than the poker game, is that Benny and Franco have the same lawyer. Everyone seems to have secrets. That's never good where money's involved, especially when you're dealing with an underground business like the one Benny was running."

Amanda nodded, seemingly lost in thought. "Well, big guy, you've got quite a web of intrigue to unravel, don't you?"

She reached out her hand and held mine, rubbing my knuckles with her thumb.

"I know this is important to you, Harry. And I know you'll figure it out. Is there anything I can do to help?"

That wasn't a hollow offer. She and her analytical way of thinking had helped me solve more cases than I can count. But it was Christmas, and I didn't want to get her involved. She had better things to do with her time. It was enough that she was willing to listen to me ramble on.

So, we shifted the conversation to family. I ordered

more drinks—two was my limit because I still had work to do—and we discussed what we were going to do with our time off.

I'd planned to rest and enjoy a little time with my family. My father, August, wanted to play golf the day after Christmas, but I wasn't sure I was up for that. The riverfront course can be a real bear in mid-winter. Amanda and I were both looking forward to the time off together so I let her take the reins, knowing she'd make sure we'd have a happy time.

She talked about the gifts she'd already purchased, including a new golf bag for my father and a day at the spa for Maria. There it was again, the spa. Was I receiving some kind of message? Maybe. Be that as it may, the pleasant moment inevitably drew to a close. It was time to go back to work. Which I did, feeling a whole lot better than I did when I'd left the office just over an hour earlier.

Chapter Twenty-Nine

Thursday 2pm

Thirty minutes later, Kate picked me up at the office and we headed to the Diego Trejo residence primarily to interview his brother and wife. Interviewing a family member is never easy, especially on the heels of someone's violent death, but it has to be done.

Kate drove us to the cabinet shop where he'd worked and lived—Samson safely secured in the back seat.

"He lived above the shop," Kate said when I questioned her. "You'd better let me take this one, but feel free to jump in whenever you feel the need."

"Fine," I said as we exited the car. It was a nice day; a little chilly, but the sun was shining and I was feeling pretty good.

We entered the shop to be immediately assailed by noise and a strong smell of a mixture of wood stain, paint thinner and sawdust.

It was a busy shop. There were at least a dozen people, all males, working with a variety of hand and power tools:

saws, sanders, staple guns, reupholstering soft furniture, repairing and refinishing tables, sideboards, antique desks, dressers, you name it. They all seemed committed to the task at hand. But, when Kate and I walked in, the place went quiet—hand tools were turned off—and we received some shifty looks, and I had to wonder why. Did we really look that obvious? It didn't bode well for our interview.

Kate held up her badge, approached the nearest worker —who'd been sanding a tabletop—and shoved it in his face, her badge, not the sander, and asked where she could find Manuel Trejo, Diego's brother.

The worker glared at her for a moment, pointed to a glass-paneled wall at the back of the shop, then went back to work.

Manuel was in his office. We carefully made our way through the shop and Kate knocked on the door, grabbed the knob, pushed it open and stepped inside.

Though the main area of the shop had once been a warehouse—concrete floors and a high ceiling—the office was... almost opulent: clean, tidy with a beautiful oak desk and matching bookcases along the back wall. The hardwood floor was a little scuffed in places, but it shone brightly under the overhead lights.

Manuel was seated at the desk, tapping with two fingers on the keyboard of an iMac computer. He didn't even bother to look up when we entered.

"Manuel Trejo," Kate said, holding up her badge. "I'm Captain Gazzara, Chattanooga Police. This is Harry Starke. We're here to talk to you about your brother, Diego."

Manuel stopped tapping. He looked up, rolled his chair back a little and nodded slowly.

"Please. Sit down." He nodded at one of the two chairs in front of the desk.

He looked pretty fit and judging by his biceps, obviously worked out. But I figured that no matter how much weight he benched, he was unlikely to fill out his narrow frame any further. He had soft brown eyes, curly hair, a narrow face and wore a thin mustache, a pen tucked behind his ear and a sour expression on his face. He wasn't pleased to see us.

"I already know my brother is dead," he growled. There was no hint of regret in his voice. "So what is it you want to tell me?"

"I don't want to tell you anything," Kate replied sharply. "I want to ask you some questions."

"So go ahead and ask," he snapped back. "I know nothing."

"When did you last talk to your brother?" she asked.

"Last night."

"What time?" she asked. "Where?"

"About nine. He came over to my place to pick up an ethernet cable."

"And?" Kate snapped.

"And what?"

"Manuel," she said. "We're trying to find out what happened to your brother. Now you can either talk to us here or you can do it at the police department. Which is it to be?"

He glanced from her to me, then back at her.

"He got a phone call." He shrugged.

"Who did he speak to? Did he say?" Kate asked.

"No!"

"Do you have any idea who it might have been?" she asked.

"No... I don't know half the people my brother wasted his time with. He was *el perdedor*, a loser... Always broke. I had to support him. He lived here, over the shop." He looked up at the ceiling. "He was nervous... about the person he talked to last night. He wouldn't tell me what it was about, and I didn't want to know. He always had these crazy stories about how he was going to make it big, but he never did. I loved my brother but..."

Interesting, I thought. *Diego didn't have a phone on him when...*

"Was your brother an honest man, Manuel?" Kate asked.

Manuel looked her up and down as if somehow she had disgusted him. Then he grabbed a bottle from his desktop and gulped down a copious amount of water.

"We're all honest people," he said, throwing the empty bottle neatly into the trash can halfway across the room. "We Trejos, we work hard. But some of us are more honest than others." He spat out his last remark like it was a nasty taste in his mouth. Clearly, turmoil and hostility were problems for the Trejo family.

"Do you know Franco de Luca?" she asked.

He nodded slowly and said, "I know of him. He is... not an honest man."

"Could that phone call he received have been from de Luca?" she asked.

"Of course. It could have been from anybody. How would I know?"

"Did you know he went after de Luca with a gun last night?" she said.

He looked shocked. "No, I didn't."

"Why did he do that, d'you suppose?"

"I don't know," he replied.

He shifted in his chair, then stood and walked out from behind his desk. He was shorter than I expected, but my eyes were drawn to his hip. He was packing. It was a .45, a 1911, stainless steel with staghorn grips.

Why would the owner of a woodshop need to carry a weapon like that? I wondered.

He opened a box on the credenza to his right, took out a fat cigar, bit off the tip, spat it out, returned to his desk and lit it, puffing out huge clouds of smoke.

"Did you know about the poker games?" Kate asked.

"What poker games?"

"Diego was a regular member of a poker game played each week at the Sorbonne," she replied.

"I did not know that. He had no money for poker."

"Did you know he was trading information?" she said.

He frowned, narrowed his eyes and said, "Information? What are you talking about?"

"He was selling sensitive information," Kate said, then hesitated and waited for him to answer.

The trouble was, we didn't know what information Diego was selling, or if he was indeed selling it.

"Bullshit," Manuel snapped. "Diego was not that smart."

"How's the rest of the family handling your brother's death?" I asked.

He turned to look at me. It wasn't a friendly look.

"His wife and kids, they are inconsolable. What do you think? They are in Mexico. I called her. She loved him but... she left him and went to live with her mother and father. I don't see them often. Consuela, she told me she would come to the funeral. I have to pay for her to come, and for the funeral."

"When did she leave him?" I asked.

He shrugged, then said, "One year ago, a little more maybe."

"Did he ever talk to her?" I asked.

He shook his head. "Once in a while. Not often."

I wasn't sure if that was true or not. His evasiveness was beginning to wear on me.

"And your brother worked here?" Kate asked.

"*Si*, Diego worked here, sometimes. He did odd jobs. Mostly fixing furniture for anyone who would pay him."

"How much did he make doing that?" she asked.

"Enough."

Kate took a stab at a few more questions, but the longer we spoke to him, the more Manuel clammed up.

"Did your brother have any enemies?" she asked.

He let out a sigh of exasperation, leaned back in his chair and put his hands on his hips, exposing the gun.

"Listen to me, *si*? I don't want to speculate on who my brother did or did not get along with. I have my opinions of some of the people he knew. They were all losers. But I'm not going to... how you say, throw anyone under the bus just so you can jump on them and lock them up."

With that, he folded his arms across his chest, his cigar clamped firmly between his lips. A not-so-subtle way of telling us he was done talking.

He was hiding something, all right. He was sitting on the fence along with everyone we'd spoken with so far.

Kate and I took the hint, told him goodbye and told him that we'd probably want to talk to him again.

He just grunted in reply and we left him sitting there staring after us.

It was as we walked back through the shop that it really started to hit me. Every one of Manuel's employees stood still and glared at us. I'd had people staring daggers at me before. As a PI, it came with the territory. But the way these people were staring at us made me feel like they were ready to jump us.

"Was it me," Kate asked as she drove out of the parking lot, "or did it feel like we were walking through a forest of killers?"

"It wasn't just you," I replied.

She was right, and it wasn't just the part of town we were in.

"What the hell d'you think is going on there?" she asked.

I didn't know.

Chapter Thirty

Thursday Afternoon 3pm

It was just after three when Kate dropped me off at my offices that afternoon. The day had turned dark again and it was beginning to rain. I sat at my desk with a cup of coffee, listening to the raindrops pattering against the window.

I hadn't been there but a couple of moments, enjoying the quiet, when there was a knock at my door and Tim and TJ walked in.

"How did you know I was back?" I asked. *As if I don't know.*

"Jacque called me," TJ said, grinning.

"So," I said. "Sit down. Talk to me."

And they did. They sat down opposite my desk. Tim pulled his chair closer so he could put his gear on the desktop.

"Check this out, Harry," TJ said, handing Tim his iPad, who passed it over to me.

"Tim did most of the work, but we found Porter."

"Really? You sure this is him?" I asked as I looked at the screen.

Jeffery Porter: Age 35, born in Phoenix, Arizona.

"Oh yeah. It's him, all right," Tim said. "I did a nation-wide search through various databases, as you suggested, including the DMV, and we found him."

I looked at the driver's license photo and compared it with the screenshot from the poker game. Tim was right. It was definitely him. Even in the DL photo I could see a deep, shark-like energy in his eyes.

I looked at Tim. "You didn't... No! Forget it. I don't want to know."

"He has no criminal record," Tim said, avoiding my eyes, "and that driver's license is all the information we have: no credit card information, no bank accounts, nothing. So, there's no way of finding his current address... or anything."

"Still, awesome job, guys," I said. "Don't worry. We'll find him. I'm sure of it. It's just a matter of time."

I studied the driver's license. "This license is current. There's an address here, in Phoenix. Maybe he has family there? Have you tried to contact them?"

"I did," Tim replied. Then, reading from his notes, "It's a PO box registered to Jeffery Porter. He opened it three years ago in December of 2015, paid five years rent up front, and hasn't been back since. The address they have for him is a rental property. He left that address on January 31, seven weeks after he opened the PO box. The phone number he gave them when he opened it is disconnected. He's a ghost."

"So," I said thoughtfully. "Here we have a guy from Arizona who's living off the record... What's he doing here in Chattanooga?"

"Drugs, maybe?" Tim suggested.

"Hmm, possibly," I replied.

TJ leaned forward, pointed to the iPad, and said, "Go to the next screen. I found something else. I made some notes for you to read. I think it confirms your 'Benny has a tech-savvy partner' theory."

I tapped the screen, and sure enough, according to TJ, there was no record anywhere of Benny buying the equipment that was installed in his secret room.

"What he had in there is specialized stuff: spy stuff. You can't just buy gear like that locally. Tim and I, we both looked into it, and we found there are only a handful of suppliers here in the US that carry it."

I handed the iPad back to Tim, who handed it back to TJ.

"So, we're clear that he didn't shop at Radio Shack for his cameras."

Tim and TJ both chuckled.

"Well, if Benny did purchase it, he must have done so online, right?" I asked.

They both nodded.

"And since you couldn't find any record of that," I continued, "someone else must have done so."

Again, they both nodded.

"Then who the hell was it?" I asked, more of myself than Tim and TJ.

"Do you think it was one of the players?" TJ asked.

"I don't think so," I replied. "It wouldn't make sense for them both to be at the table... Would it? Whoever installed those cameras would have known they were on and would've kept clear of them, right?"

They both nodded.

"And why didn't the cameras record audio along with the footage?" I said. "That makes no sense at all."

"I have a theory about that, Harry," Tim said.

"Oh, yes? Do tell."

"I've been digging into the video files on my desktop. Harry, I think some of the older recordings did have audio. I think Benny pulled the mics. I checked the input and output information, and the cameras do have the ability to record sound."

"That's an interesting discovery," I said. "Why wasn't he using it?"

"I don't know," Tim said. "But I do have some screenshots and photos I can send over to the police department, if that's okay."

"Sure," I said.

"Harry," Tim continued, "I'd like to take another look at that secret room. D'you think that would be okay?"

"Of course. I'll arrange it with Kate. What exactly is it you're looking for?"

"Dunno," he replied and pushed his glasses further up the bridge of his nose. "I guess I'll know it when I see it."

I nodded and called Kate. She answered on the first ring. "What's up, Harry?"

"Tim wants to take another look at the concealed room. Do you have a problem with that?"

"Of course not. When does he want to do it?"

I looked across my desk at Tim and asked him. He shrugged and said, "Tomorrow, around eight-thirty?"

I put the phone on speaker and said, "You're on speaker, Kate. Did you hear that?"

"Yep! Tim, I'll have someone meet you there and let you into the office. What d'you expect to find?"

"I don't know... Something, maybe nothing..."

"Okay," she said, cutting him off. She knows Tim almost as well as I do. "Eight-thirty tomorrow morning. That it, Harry?"

"Yes, talk to you tomorrow. Have a good one." And with that I hung up.

"Okay, gentlemen," I said, rising to my feet and stretching my arms behind my back. "If you don't mind, I'm going to call it a day. I need to go home and be with my family."

Traffic was slow, thanks to rush hour and the weather. It was a little after four. The skies were already dark, and it was raining, a fine drizzle. I was hoping I'd make it home in time to spend some time with Jade before dinner, something I rarely got to do those last few days before Christmas.

Jade was eighteen months old now, and already she looked much more like her mother than she did me. She had Amanda's eyes, hair color, and her nose. Everyone tried to make me feel better by telling me she had my chin, but I couldn't really see it, and I hoped to God she didn't.

Whoever she took after, Jade had changed both our lives so much, and for the better. I doubted she'd remember anything about that Christmas. I sure as hell couldn't remember my life as a toddler. But I wanted it to be special for her.

As I drove up Scenic Highway, I thought about Trish Hinkle, and Diego Trejo's children. Both had just lost their father. I found it very sad, and not just because of the season. Not every parent deserves a child, but every child deserves a parent. These kids had lost someone important to them, and... Well, regardless of what their parents were or did, I felt a twinge in my heart for them.

By the time I made the turn onto East Brow, my thoughts had turned to my own situation and the times I'd almost lost my life. It kind of put things into perspective for me.

I didn't want Jade to grow up without me. I'd never thought it was something I needed to worry about, but I was a family man and things had changed.

Chapter Thirty-One

Friday Morning 9:30am

I entered my house through the garage door into the kitchen. The place smelled like a giant cookie—Willie Wonka's Chocolate Factory. Rose, Maria, and Amanda must have made several hundred cookies in a dozen different varieties. They were everywhere: gingerbread, peanut butter, oatmeal, sugar cookies and more.

Amanda welcomed me with a soft kiss on the lips and a glass of Laphroaig in my hand, then ushered me off into the living room where Jade and Maria were sitting on the floor in front of the television watching *Frosty the Snowman*. I sat down on the floor beside Jade. She didn't even know I was there; she was transfixed.

Was I disappointed? No! Of course not, because when the movie was over, she turned around and crawled up into my lap. Nice!

Dinner that evening was also nice. Nice and quiet; no talk of work, just pleasant family chatter. I was in bed by ten and asleep by five after.

I rose early again the following morning with time for a short run and a good breakfast; then I told my family good-bye, grabbed a tin of mixed cookies and headed out down the mountain. It was a glorious day. The sky was clear, the sun was just peeping up over the horizon and all was well with the world... at least I thought it was.

It was a little before eight-thirty when I walked into the lobby and from there to the break room where I left the cookies for everyone to enjoy, made myself some coffee, grabbed several cookies—knowing that when I returned later in the day they'd already be eaten up—and then went to my office.

The pressure at Starke Investigations was easing a little. My staff had managed to close a half-dozen cases over the past several weeks, so I was feeling a little better about devoting my time to Benny's case.

It had been a long and... yes, fruitful year, and we were all in good spirits. We were all still tired, but we had the week between Christmas and the New Year to recuperate.

I was still drinking my coffee and ruminating over what had happened during the past year when my phone buzzed in my pocket. I had a text from Kate.

"Hey. I'll pick you up in thirty minutes. We're going to see Harris. We'll discuss along the way."

That we will! I thought as I texted her the thumbs-up sign. I was tired of being lied to. It was the time to come out swinging and get to the truth.

Kate picked me up at nine-thirty, sans Samson who had gone to the doggy daycare for the day, and we arrived at Harris's shop some fifteen minutes later. The shop was busy. Harris was flustered, even more so when we told him we had more questions for him. By the time we got him back in his office, his face was beet red.

"You can't keep doing this to me," he bleated. "You can't keep coming here trying to shake me down like this."

Oh yes, he was upset, all right. Me? I didn't give a shit. Nor, for that matter, did Kate. She did, however, take the more... diplomatic route.

"Rod, we're not trying to shake you down—" Kate began, but he cut her off.

"Yes, you are," he snapped. "You're both trying to screw with me again. You're trying to get me locked up again. Frickin' typical. You people never let go; never give a guy a break. Well this time—"

"For God's sake, Rod. Shut up and listen," I said, raising my voice.

And he did, but he glared at me, breathing hard, trying to control his temper. But, he knew better than to pick a fight with us given the circumstances.

"That's better," I said. "Now just sit down and take it easy. We have just a few questions, then we'll be out of your hair, and no, we're not trying to lock you up again. If we were, we'd have already done it."

He blew air out through his lips, then said, "What d'you want to know?"

"What exactly was going on at those poker games? What secrets were you trading?"

His mouth dropped open. His breath caught in his throat. He was aghast. "What?"

"Come on, Rod," Kate said. "We know you weren't just playing for cash. You were trading information. All of you."

"Why you... You... Who told you that?"

"Cut the act, Rod," I said, taking a step forward to put a little more pressure on him.

"We've spoken to... well, let's just say we know all about Benny's little sideline, and the money that changed hands, and that it was an exclusive little club; you had to pay to play. Now, for the last time, what was the information *you* were trading?"

He stared at me, then at Kate. I could see the rage building up inside him. He tried but couldn't control it. He lost his composure, just for a second, then recovered as best he could.

"Oh... no! No, no," he yelped. "You're not going to badger me into telling you something that will cost me my life. I'd rather go back to jail. Screw you, Starke, and you... you... I know my rights." His voice lowered with each word until he was talking normally again.

"I have the right to not answer your questions," he continued. "And, as a business owner, I have the right to tell you to get off my property."

"Rod," Kate protested.

"Enough. I'm telling you to leave. Either arrest me or leave my shop... Right now!"

Damn! Damn! That's just great. Now what?

Kate opened her mouth to speak. I figured she was going to try to talk him down, but I could see by the set of his jaw and his body language he would have none of it. So I touched her arm and nodded.

"Leave it, Captain," I said. "He's been playing in the big leagues, and now that Benny's dead, they'll want to tie up the loose ends."

I looked at Harris and said, "How does that feel, Rod, being a loose end?"

"G...g...get out of my frickin' off...fice," he stuttered.

I smiled at him, nodded and said, "Good luck, Rod." And we left him staring after us, his face red.

I turned around to wave at him, just in time to see him put his cell phone to his ear.

"How long would it take to get his cell phone records, Kate?" I asked as we got into her unmarked cruiser.

"A week, maybe more," she replied.

"Why don't you do that?" I said.

She nodded, then said, "You know, I'm getting pretty tired of being given the runaround by this group of miscreants." She shook her head and sighed.

Kate started the engine, put the car in reverse, looked over her shoulder to make sure no one was behind her when she said, "What the hell?" and put the car back into park.

"Harry, look. Look who it is."

Walking quickly across the lot, heading toward Harris's office, was a guy with a familiar face.

"That's Jeff Porter," she said, rolling down her window. "Isn't it?"

It was, and he was clearly on a mission. He marched up to the side door that led to Harris's office and banged on it until he came out. When Harris saw who it was, he completely lost his cool and took a couple of steps out of the office, both hands balled into fists.

"You!" we heard him yell. "Are you frickin' insane? What the frickin' hell are you doing here? The cops were just here, for God's sake."

He'd been riled up when we left, but now he was in one hell of a state. Then he toned it down a little and more words were exchanged.

It was hard to make out what they were saying, but after a few seconds, Rod stepped backward into his office doorway. Porter followed. It was at that point Harris turned his head and spotted us, made eye contact with me, and he froze, a look of horror on his face.

Porter saw the look on his face and turned around to see

what he was looking at, and his face fell. Unmarked or not, there's no mistaking a police cruiser.

I smiled and waggled my fingers at them. They looked like two kids caught stealing candy in the 7-11.

We both exited the car.

"Jeffery Porter," Kate called. "I'm Captain..."

But before she could finish, he took off running.

I swore and shouted at him to freeze. Of course, he didn't, so I drew in a deep breath and ran after him.

He ran across the lot, turned left onto Rossville Boulevard and hightailed it as fast as he could go, his arms pumping like pistons.

Behind me, I heard Kate start her car and peel out of the parking lot, blue lights flashing, siren shrieking. And down the street we went.

Chapter Thirty-Two

Friday Morning 10:30am

I wasn't exactly in the best shape I'd ever been. True, I'd run a couple of miles earlier that morning, but this was different. I was dressed for the cold and sprinting down the street after a younger and fitter man than I was, and I felt it... It was really messing me up. I was breathing hard, and my legs felt as if they were made of lead.

By the time Kate peeled out onto the street, he'd already made a left at East 43rd. No sooner had he made the turn than he made another left, ran alongside a deep concrete drainage ditch and disappeared into a stand of trees. I ran after him.

I was fast, but not in good enough shape to catch this guy. He was fifteen years younger and in amazing shape. The Christmas cookies I'd stuffed into my face that morning weren't helping either. My stomach was already beginning to cramp as I ran into the trees.

I heard Kate turn onto East 43rd behind me. She must have seen me disappear into the trees because she cut her siren, made a left onto 6th, then another left onto East 42nd and cut him off as he ran out of the trees. I ran up behind him, my weapon drawn. Kate was already out of her car, Glock in hand pointing straight at him. He was bent over at the waist, head down, his hands on his knees, breathing heavily.

I stood behind him for a couple of seconds, breathing hard, trying to get my breath back.

He looked up at Kate and gasped, "What the f—? I ain't done nothing. You can't arrest me. What're you arresting me for?" He shook his head and stood upright, his feet apart, hands on his hips, still breathing hard.

He was tall, five-eleven, with dark hair, cut short almost like a helmet, with loads of product. There was also a small scar on his left cheek we hadn't seen because of the camera angle.

"Who said we're here to arrest you, Jeff?" she said. "We just want to chat."

I slipped my gun into my holster and gestured down the street and said, "There's a McDonald's on East 45th. Why don't we all head in there and talk over a cup of coffee?"

Porter wasn't happy about the idea, but he was smart enough to know it was either that or he was going downtown. So, reluctantly, he accepted our invitation and climbed into the back of Kate's cruiser.

By then it was after ten, and the restaurant was almost empty. Kate placed our order while I marched him over to a corner table, far enough away from the few customers there were for us not to be heard.

He sat down and slid across the seat so he was sitting next to the window.

He sat quietly, his arms folded and a juvenile pout on his lips.

Kate brought the coffees along with three sausage and egg biscuits and, as she set them down, he said, "So this is how the police do it here, is it?"

"Sometimes," Kate replied. "Why'd you run from us, Jeff?"

He wrinkled his nose and shrugged. "Because of the way he was looking at me."

"You're from Arizona, aren't you?" I said. "What brings you to Chattanooga?"

"Work."

"And that work would be?" Kate asked and then took a sip of her coffee.

"I work for a tech company. Ravern Solutions. They transferred me out here."

Our ears perked up at that. *So he works in technology*, I thought. *Perfect!*

I made note of the name, then said, "They must pay well for you to come all this way."

He shrugged, looked down at his coffee and said, "I guess."

"So, how d'you know Rod Harris?" Kate asked, setting her cup down.

Again he shrugged and looked away to the left. "I know him from the gym."

"What gym?" I asked, sure he was lying.

He hesitated for a moment, then said, "The Sports Barn on Market Street."

"So, if we were to ask Rod, he would confirm that, right?" Kate asked.

"I guess."

"D'you play poker, Jeff?" I asked.

Again he looked away. "No."

"Oh dear," I said gently. "That's not true, is it, Jeff?"

He didn't answer.

"We know you're a member of a group that plays... or should I say, played, regularly at the Sorbonne. We have you on video, so why did you lie?"

"Because he's frickin' dead, is why. The guy who ran the game. I had nothing to do with that, I swear."

"Well, maybe you didn't, maybe you did," Kate said.

He just shook his head and looked down at the table.

"We also know that poker was just a small part of what was going on there," Kate continued. "We know the players were trading information with Benny. But you knew that too, didn't you, Jeff?"

He looked up at her, scrunching up his face and glaring at her, but all he said was, "No."

"No? Then why were you there?"

He thought for a minute, then said, seemingly choosing his words carefully, "Okay, so I work with computers, right? Well, Benny knew that—"

"How did he know?" Kate asked, interrupting him.

"I met him at the bar, the Sorbonne. I was having a drink and he asked where I was from. I told him and... well, one thing led to another, and he asked me what I did, like you did."

"Okay," Kate said. "Continue."

"Benny knew I worked with computers, right? So, now and then he'd ask me to..." He shrugged, then continued, "Look stuff up for him."

I got it. "You're a hacker," I said.

Again he shrugged but didn't answer.

"And he paid you?' I asked.

This time he nodded. "Yeah, he paid me well."

"And what sort of information did you provide him with?" Kate asked.

"Mostly financial stuff... you know... people stuff."

"What people?" I asked. "We need names."

"Nope! That's not going to happen. I tell you that and I'll be lying in the morgue alongside Benny. There's nothing you can say or do that will make me tell you that stuff."

We asked several more of the standard questions: Where were you between six and seven on the night Benny died, and so on and so forth, but we learned very little else. He thought he was winning, and he was clearly beginning to relax. His body language changed, and his answers came more quickly and with more self-assurance. But he had a dodgy way of answering personal questions. He was deceitful, evasive, and I couldn't help but wonder how much money he walked away with after the poker games.

So we decided—actually it was me who decided—to change the route, so to speak.

"Did you help Benny set up the equipment in that back room?" I asked.

"Equipment?"

"Cameras and recording equipment, yes."

The confidence he'd built up during the previous conversations deserted him. The color drained from his face. He was obviously stunned by the question.

"No," he said and looked me right in the eye. Then he picked up his coffee, finished what was left, set it down again, then leaned back and stared at us, his face set.

Did he do it, or was he merely shocked to learn that the games were being recorded? There was no way to tell, and I was pretty sure that he wasn't going to either... tell, that is.

"Jeff—" I began.

"Listen, Mr..." he said, interrupting me.

"Starke. Harry Starke."

"Yeah, that, and Captain Gazzara. You can ask me all the questions you want, but you've got absolutely nothing on me except that I played a game or two of poker and helped a friend verify certain information. There's nothing illegal about that. Banks do it all the time. You've got nothing. So, if you're not going to arrest me, I think I've said all I need to say. I have places to be."

Kate pursed her lips and gave me one of her classic *can you believe this shit?* looks.

Although he was acting smug and thought he was tough, he was correct. We did have nothing, so we had to let him go. That said, I was happier with that interview than most of the others we'd conducted. Even though he'd been careful when he answered my questions, Jeff Porter had told us more about himself and what Benny was up to than he realized.

"All right, Jeff," I said and looked at Kate for confirmation. She nodded, and I told him he was free to go.

"Thank you for your time," Kate said dryly.

Obviously eager to leave, he was up from his seat as if he'd been stung by a bee. He threw on his leather jacket and stepped out of the booth, muttered a curt thank you and turned to go... and then he stopped, turned again and took a couple of steps back until he was standing in front of us.

"Look," he said, his voice low, his tone serious, "I know you've got nothing. I'm not talking just about me. I'm talking about your case, or whatever it is you call it. You've got nothing. And, you won't get anywhere. You just won't, believe me. Even if you thought you did. But let me give you a bit of advice, Mr. Starke. Back away from this. I mean it. You don't know who you're messing with."

Then he left without saying another word.

"Well now, wasn't he just charming?" Kate scoffed and rolled her eyes.

"D'you believe him?" I asked. "The warning, I mean?"

She shook her head and nibbled on some French fries she'd ordered. "Nope! Do you?"

I didn't answer. The truth was, I did believe him. The kid was a hacker and he obviously knew a whole lot more than he was telling.

"Did you see how he reacted when you brought up the cameras?" she asked. "He looked devastated. What d'you think, Harry. Did he install those cameras for Benny?"

"I don't know," I replied. "I don't know if we're supposed to interpret his reaction as an admission that he did install the cameras, or the fear that he might have said something he shouldn't. I wonder how Tim's doing? He's trying to recover the sound."

"It may be a little of both," Kate said thoughtfully. "Maybe he was hoping we wouldn't find the cameras."

I picked up my cup and finished my now lukewarm coffee.

"Either way," I said as I replaced the cup on the table, "and even with that ominous warning, he was undeniably scared by how much we knew."

"Aren't they all?" she replied. "They act out. They're cocky. Think they know it all. They think we're just dumb cops. But they're wrong. They don't realize just how thorough we are, that it's our job to dig deep and find their little secrets."

"True enough," I replied. "Damn it, Kate. Talk about dumb cops. We forgot to get his address."

"Not a problem," she replied. "We know where he works so we can track him down that way."

I shook my head. "It was a rookie mistake and one we

shouldn't have made. I wish Heather was nearby so we could have her tail him. Kate, there's something off about Jeffery Porter. He has no past, at least none that Tim can find, so far anyway. If he has a criminal record, he's frighteningly good at covering it up, which makes me wonder if it's his real name. That he has computer skills tends to confirm that. Think how easy it would be for a skilled hacker to erase his past and start over, and that, Kate, makes it even more unsettling. Hell, the guy can just disappear whenever he wants to. Skip town, head out of state and start over. I want him back."

"You're speculating, Harry," she replied. "Maybe you're right, but it's one heck of a leap."

I sighed. "Maybe, but you've got to admit he was right about one thing: we have *nothing!* None of our suspects are jumping off the page. None of them will talk. We're making no progress at all."

"That's not quite true, Harry," Kate said. "Four days ago we had six unidentified suspects. Now we know all but one. We also know Benny was into something that got him killed, and we know that someone big is involved. Someone Porter's afraid of."

"Maybe we should be, too," I replied, only half joking.

"Maybe we should, Harry. Maybe you're right. We still don't know as much as I would like, and that worries me, but we'll handle it. We'll move on, and we'll catch the person who killed Benny."

I looked at my watch. It was almost noon and I needed to get back to the office. It was Friday. Tuesday was Christmas Eve.

Time was running out!

Chapter Thirty-Three

Friday Afternoon 12:45pm

What little was left of the morning passed by quite slowly, which was a good thing because I needed time to think.

Jeffery Porter was a strange little punk, but he was important to the case because he obviously knew how to weasel his way into a seat at the poker table. A table with a collection of mature and connected criminals from the darkest corners of Chattanooga's underbelly. *How the hell did he do that?* I wondered. *What was his connection to the other five? Hmm... I shook my head. We need a break; something to unlock this mess. And who was Porter warning us about? Himself? Perhaps, though seeing his mask slip makes me think he isn't as confident as he would have us believe. And Franco; what about him? Hmm... He's... interesting. Maybe we should go mess with him again.*

Are they all working individually, or are they planning something together? And we still haven't put a name to that woman's face yet. She appears to be the least involved in the game. She didn't bet as often or as big as the others, and she had the least to say... Who the hell is she and what's her game, I wonder? She's... What? Boring? But boring doesn't mean she isn't pulling some strings.

"Geez, Benny," I muttered. "What the hell were you thinking? Why couldn't you have just gotten yourself killed by a drunk? Something simple so we could catch the bastard and lock him away and deal with your death in peace." I looked up at the ceiling and said, "Listen to me, you fat little son of a bitch. If you can hear me... Ah, what's the use?" I shook my head and went back to the matter at hand.

I was done pestering his daughter, Trish. I couldn't for the life of me imagine what else she could tell us, unless she'd been lying to us all along. No. My gut instincts were telling me that Trish Hinkle was an honest woman.

I sighed and gave it up. I rose to my feet and went to the breakroom for some coffee and was lucky enough to find two snowflake sugar cookies left. They looked lonely there by themselves on the plate, so I rescued them and instead of making coffee, I made a cup of Earl Grey tea; a rare choice for me, but when I was at a low point, it hit the spot. I was actually dunking a cookie in my tea when my door opened.

"Harry?"

"What is it, Jacque?" I asked, my cookie suspended over the cup.

"Bill Perks is here to see you. Do you want to talk to him?"

Deep down my gut was telling her to go ahead and talk to him, but my brain was telling me something else. "Send him in, Jacque."

He swirled into my office like a miniature tornado, slick suit, bow tie and all. Jacque following on behind.

"Mr. Starke, I'm here for an update," he said as he

collapsed into one of my chairs. *Geez, and good afternoon to you too.*

"Well. Come on. Fill me in," he snapped. "What do you know that I don't?"

I was biting my tongue so hard I'm surprised I didn't cut it in half.

"Well, Mr. Perks," I said, "even though you represent the Hinkles, I don't owe you an explanation, and I don't need to update you and, quite frankly, I don't like your attitude."

"Good effort, Starke," he replied with a smirk, "but I'm not leaving yet. And FYI, you may think you don't owe me an explanation or an update, but I'm here to tell you that yes, you do."

I couldn't mask the look of contempt I gave him.

"Oh, yes? And why is that?"

"As I am the executor of Mr. Hinkle's estate, and it was his dying wish that I hire you to catch his killer, and I have a right to updates when I ask for them. I'm also authorized to give you more money, if need be, so I think it would be prudent for us to find a better way to communicate with one another, don't you?"

What had Benny called him in his final video? A viper?

I had to give credit where it was due. The title he'd given the man sitting across from me described him perfectly. The sound of his voice made my skin crawl. And, he was sweating. I'd heard lawyers described as "greasy" before, but this guy... I closed my eyes for a second, took a breath, then leaned forward and put my hands together on top of my desk.

"Fine," I said, locking eyes with him—not a pleasant thing to do, but what the hell. "But before I tell you what's been going on, I need to clear up a few things, so I have a couple of questions for you."

"I'm all ears."

"What exactly did you know about Benny's... sideline?"

"Nothing. He didn't confide in me."

"But you did know about his revenue stream, his bank accounts, and the money? He had a lot of money. Close to two million dollars. You must have known about that."

He smirked and shook his head. "Even if I did, I couldn't talk to you about it. Attorney-client privilege."

"Oh, come on, Perks... Okay, tell me this, if you can. You knew he was up to something shady, right?"

He just shook his head slowly and smiled. A self-satisfied grin, similar to the one Jeff Porter had gifted me with only a few hours ago. However, the one on Perks' face didn't look as if it would be slipping off any time soon.

"Client privilege," he repeated, "and all that mumbo jumbo people like you hate to hear. I can't tell you anything, Mr. Starke. I'm sorry. But, if it makes you feel any better, I'll tell you this. I did not know about the poker games. So now tell me. Do you think it was one of them that killed Benny?"

"I can't tell you that," I said, playing him at his own game. Then I relented and said, "I really don't know. Benny was playing a shady game, and it wasn't poker. But I think it got him killed."

I answered several more of his questions. Most of them about the state of the investigation. Nothing seemed to surprise him. He asked his questions then sat there, listening to the answers with a smug, arrogant expression on his face.

"You don't seem shocked by what I've learned about your client," I remarked.

"Oh, I find it shocking, Mr. Starke. But it's not my job to

judge my clients. Making deductions about their character is your area of expertise. I simply wanted to know if you were any closer to finding his killer, which quite obviously, you aren't." He took a handkerchief from the inside pocket of his jacket, wiped his brow with it, and then returned it to his pocket.

I stared at him. He was still sweating. I thought he looked paler than the last time I saw him.

"Are you all right, Bill? Can I get you something? Some water, perhaps?"

The questions seemed to strike a nerve.

He glowered at me. "I'm just fine, thank you," he snapped.

"Well, if you don't have any more questions for me, I... respectfully ask you to leave. I have a lot to get done before the holiday, and my team and I are spread thin."

He nodded. "Of course, Mr. Starke. I've already taken up too much of your valuable time. And please forgive me for showing up here without warning."

I didn't say anything.

He exhaled. "I'll call ahead next time. I write contracts for a living. I should follow the rules, shouldn't I?"

Your job isn't just about following the rules, you shyster, I thought savagely. *It's about bending them.*

That ten-minute conversation with Bill Perks reminded me why I absolutely loathed the very nature of his profession.

Finally, with no little difficulty, he struggled out of the chair and onto his feet.

"I'll bid you goodbye for now, then, Harry, and look forward to our next meeting, but please do try to keep me informed." And with that he left.

I reached into my desk drawer and took out my iPad

and the flash drive Tim had given me earlier. I plugged it in and mentally thanked the kid for having the foresight to catalog the videos. I watched a couple of games at five times normal speed. I started with the first game played some nine weeks earlier. Everyone looked fresh-faced and enthusiastic except Benny, who looked nervous enough to pee his pants. By the time an hour had passed—some twelve minutes my time—around the middle of the game, the players, even Benny, seemed to have developed a rhythm. Everyone was talking. It looked like a normal poker game. I pulled up the last game they played just two weeks earlier.

I saw nothing out of the ordinary.

Which one of you did it? I wondered as I put the video into slow motion and looked around the circle. *Or was it even any of you?*

We'd been assuming... No, I'd been assuming it was one of the players... if not Benny's secret partner. But it could have been anyone or none of them, and I had to wonder if we didn't need to widen our search. And if so, how? Where should we look next?

Then again, my gut was telling me there was still something out of whack about the entire situation. Nothing was sitting right with me.

Chapter Thirty-Four

Friday Afternoon 3pm

After my somewhat discouraging encounter with Bill Perks, attorney at law, I figured I needed to steer the Hinkle investigation in a new direction.

So, that afternoon I called everyone together in the conference room. It was time to go over what we'd found, if anything, and any theories they might have. I called Kate and asked her to join us, and she agreed.

She arrived all in a rush, saying, "Sorry I'm late, everyone. I was with Corbin. He dropped me off."

"Take a seat, Kate," I said. "I'll drive you to the PD when we're done, okay?"

She nodded and sat down at the end of the table.

I turned to TJ and said, "Okay, TJ. You have the floor."

"Thanks. I wanted to talk about this because I have a feeling that something weird is going on, but I can't figure out what it is. I don't know if I'm missing something. I've been staring at tables and spreadsheets for days now."

Tim helped him cast his iPad screen to the monitor.

TJ shook his head and laughed. "Geez, what are they going to come up with next?"

Tim just grinned at him and sat down again.

"So," TJ continued. "I've been going through everyone's financials, bank accounts, credit card statements, things of that nature, and I'm not seeing anything out of the ordinary. No ATM activity. No big deposits or withdrawals. No big credit card charges. Nothing."

He showed us the financial numbers for each of the players we'd been able to identify, then rubbed his eyes.

"I know in my gut that something's not quite kosher," he continued, "but I'm damned if I can figure out what it is. If something illegal has been going on, I'm not seeing it."

TJ's our numbers guy, among other things. If he couldn't figure out what was amiss, it wasn't likely the rest of us would be much help. Still, I had a thought in the back of my mind that wasn't going away.

"Here's what I'm thinking," I said as I cast my iPad to the screen and pulled up the footage from the final poker game. "Everyone in this room that we know of is a criminal, bearing in mind we still don't know who the woman is. They're all involved in something illegal, and they're all at the table bartering information or tips. The unfortunate thing is none of these videos have audio, so whatever they're talking about is going to remain a mystery to us unless we can persuade one of them to tell us."

"It's no surprise they're all tight-lipped about what they're into," Kate said. "No one wants to be a snitch."

"Unless they're getting paid for it," TJ said.

"Actually, I wanted to address this," Tim piped up. "As you know, Harry, I went to look at the scene again." He paused for a second, flipped through several screens on his iPad, sucked in his bottom lip, let it go with a pop and then did that thing with his glasses.

"I spent two hours in that room. I went over the walls with a black light. This time I knew what I was looking for. Anyway, I found evidence of two possible microphones. One in the vent where they found the safe. It had been well hidden, and I probably wouldn't have found it had it not been jerked out of there. I found where the other had been in the hole that houses the door lock, behind the brass plate. That one was brilliant. The problem is, they all must have been wireless because when they were removed, it killed the audio. Can I see your iPad, please, Harry?"

I slid it over to him, and he pulled up the file information on the footage for us to see.

"The video not having audio didn't have anything to do with the level of encryption as I first thought. It was because the two microphones had been pulled more than thirty days prior to these recordings. So, that's why all we have is the camera feed."

"So that means Benny's partner would have been able to listen in on the games before someone pulled the mics. Why would someone do that? And a *month* before Benny was murdered?"

"To protect someone in the room?" Jacque suggested. "Or all of them... Maybe that was when they actually started peddling information."

"Or," Heather offered, "whoever removed them knew something sensitive was going to be discussed and didn't want it on the record."

"We spoke with Jeff Porter today," Kate said. "He all but confirmed that there was someone other than Benny pulling the strings, and he warned us off."

"That narrows it down," TJ said dryly. He shook his

head. TJ isn't the most patient man on the planet. He's great with numbers, but he's a man of action and he can be dangerous.

"If it was Benny that pulled the mics," I said, "we may never know, or why. Maybe it wasn't him. I can't see it being one of the players; they wouldn't have known about them—"

"Unless one of them was the puppet master," TJ interrupted me. "And I'm thinking it's the woman."

I nodded and continued, "I think this puppet master, as you call him... or her." I looked pointedly at TJ. He grinned. I continued, "I think he ordered Diego Trejo to take out Franco de Luca. What d'you think about that? Anyone?"

Silence.

"I think you really know how to ask the hard questions, Harry," Kate said after a while.

"So, this is the direction I think we should go," I said. "We need to find out who's running this... this Legion of Doom and shut it down at the source." I looked at Tim. He grinned at me and poked his glasses.

"And the woman; she's bugging the hell out of me. Who is she and why is she there? We need to find out. Any leads, Tim? If you have any leads, now's the time to share them."

"I'm working on it, Harry," he replied, "but I have nothing so far. She's a ghost. Other than facial recognition..."

"Don't even go there," I said. "Anyone else?"

"Could she be someone from Benny's past?" Jacque asked. "Maybe she's another of his relatives we didn't know about."

"That's a bit of a shot in the dark," Kate said.

"Maybe," Jacque replied, "but I think it's worth a look. After all, he kept his daughter a secret all these years. Maybe the woman is his mother."

I knew she was joking, and I laughed, but I also knew she could be right.

I nodded and said, "Tim, take a look into it, but don't waste a lot of time on it. I'm doubtful he had any more family members we don't know about, and even if he did, it's even more doubtful they'd be involved in something like this."

Tim nodded and I said, "I want you all to go home and think about it over the weekend. Time is short. It will be Christmas Eve on Tuesday, and I'm frustrated as hell. It's no one's fault. We're just up against a rock wall. The longer it takes to crack this thing, the more time these people have to conspire together and cover their tracks. Two men are already dead. We need to stop them before this thing escalates out of hand."

We talked it round and round for another fifteen minutes or so and got nowhere.

Me? I was... beyond frustrated, though I didn't let my team see it... at least I don't think I did.

In the end, I stood up and clapped my hands. "Meeting over, folks. Go on home, all of you. Have a nice weekend, get some rest and come back on Monday morning invigorated and ready to change the world."

They all rose except Kate who remained seated staring at me. She's known me a long time, longer than anyone else at the table, and I could tell she knew how frustrated I was.

TJ was the last to leave the room. He was about to walk out the door when I called him back.

"TJ," I said. "Bill Perks. I want you to look into his finances."

"Perks? Why him?"

The truth was, I really didn't know. What I did know was that we needed to broaden our search. And...

"He stormed into my office a couple of hours ago and—" I said before TJ interrupted me.

"And you think that's a good reason for me to waste my time, right?"

I shook my head and smiled at him. "You do tell it like it is, don't you, TJ?"

He didn't answer.

"No," I said, "that's not it at all. I don't know why, but I had the feeling that he was trying to insert himself into the investigation."

"Which," Kate added, "is often something the guilty do. They do it to divert attention away from themselves and to keep tabs on what the police are doing so they can cover their tracks."

I shrugged. "Look, I'm not saying Perks is guilty of anything, but he was Benny's lawyer and he is Franco de Luca's, and that's as good a reason as any to take a closer look at him."

Kate and TJ stared at me.

I shrugged and said, "Hands up all who don't agree." And grinned at them both.

Neither of them raised their hands.

Chapter Thirty-Five

Friday Afternoon 5:30pm

While my concerns still hadn't melted away by the end of the day, I was able to distract myself by finding a Christmas gift for Amanda.

Now me... I have absolutely no talent for that kind of thing. I needed help so I called Jacque into the mix, and she, along with Kate, helped me figure it out. I had to have it shipped FedEx to make sure it would arrive on time, but it was worth it just to get it off my mind. Oh, don't get me wrong. I knew she'd love it, and it really was a huge weight off my chest.

That done, it was time for me to take Kate back to the PD and her car; she had to go pick Samson up from the doggie daycare. I told her she should have brought him with her. Yeah, I do. I like dogs. I even had one for a short time, a little Jack Russell terrier I rescued from a crazed woman on Signal Mountain. That was when I was dealing with the case of Chief Johnston's missing daughter. That woman almost killed me. If it hadn't been for... Well, that's another story. The dog's name, by the way, was Merry. I kept her for... I dunno. Six months maybe. But she was not getting any exercise and I hated having to leave her in her kennel all day, so I gave her to Wendy, Jacque's partner in life... and that's yet another story.

Anyway, I wished everyone a good night and an even better weekend, and I set out to take Kate to the police department on Amnicola Highway so she could retrieve her car.

It was rush hour on a Friday, so you can imagine what the traffic was like. So we had plenty of time to talk about the upcoming holidays. Kate stated she was going to do nothing for a week. She was going to lie around the apartment with Samson. She'd already been out and purchased a half-dozen chicken breasts and some rib-eye steaks to go with his kibbles, and I had to smile.

Kate is an inordinately beautiful woman. She's five-eleven, forty-one, with tawny blond hair, a high forehead, an oval face with high cheekbones and huge hazel eyes. She has a slender figure, works out and loves to run. But she's single. No boyfriend. Oh she's had a few, but none of them measured up. There was a time when she and I... but that's yet another story and I won't go into it here, and no, she's not gay; that I can personally attest to.

So what was I smiling at? Here we have this incredible, successful woman and she spends her time alone... except for her newly acquired partner, Samson. Oh don't get me wrong. He's a good-looking fella and he already loves her, and she him, but here it was, almost Christmas and she was quite happy to spend it with a dog. I asked her to come and spend Christmas Day with us, but she turned me down, saying she needed to rest.

Well, I was going to see that she did. She didn't know it yet, but I'd ordered her a case of Cabernet Sauvignon from the Figgins Estate: nice! I intended to present it to her on Christmas Eve.

"What did you get Samson for Christmas?" I asked.

"So far, not much: just some chewy bones and some treats. Hmm, to be honest, I hadn't thought much about it."

The conversation tapered off as we drew closer to the police department. The car had finally warmed up enough that I didn't feel as if I was sitting in a refrigerator.

I turned left onto Riverfront Drive, eased up on the speed, and said, "I appreciate everything you're doing to help solve this, Kate."

"Thanks..."

Her tone was off. Yes, Kate and I had dated in the past, and now we were best friends, so it wasn't difficult for me to see she was working up to say something difficult. Something she wasn't quite sure how to say.

"Harry, I'm worried."

"About? The case? It'll work out. It might—"

"No," she said, interrupting me. "It's not that I'm worried about. It's you. Some of your theories..." Her voice trailed off.

I was... stunned. I kept my hands on the wheel and stared out through the windshield, but I could feel my face growing hot. I didn't get it.

"I thought we were on the same page," I said. "All of us."

"Don't get me wrong, Harry, we're getting there, and I really do think we'll crack this thing, eventually, but, this Legion of Doom thing seems to really be getting to you."

"Kate, that was a joke, for Pete's sake."

"I'm aware, Harry. But that doesn't change the fact that

209

you're fixating on this group. Not everything's a conspiracy."

The traffic had thinned, but I was becoming a little perturbed by a blue Honda CRV. It was riding my bumper with its headlights on bright. I sped up, waiting for a chance to merge into another lane and gain some distance.

"Benny's murder was horrible," she continued, "and we know a lot more about him than we did, but we can't let—"

"I get it," I replied, interrupting her. "Not everything is a conspiracy. Until it is."

Kate started to protest, but I cut her off.

"Until someone like Shady puts a bomb in your office, and kidnaps Jacque, and does some serious damage to you and the people you love."

"Whoa, Harry. Now look..."

A temper valve burst inside my head. It wasn't so much what she said as it was the clown in the Honda hugging my tail.

"No, you look," I said. "I understand you think I'm taking it all too seriously, but that's the way it's going to be. Porter meant what he said, and I'm going to believe it until I have a solid reason to think otherwise!" I was talking a mile a minute.

"Whoa!"

"Kate! Stop yelling—"

"I'm not yelling at you!" she shouted. "Look out!"

The blue Honda that had been on my tail had suddenly switched lanes and was closing on me fast. He barreled up alongside me and swerved toward me. I wrenched the wheel to the right and rode the hard shoulder.

"*Son of a bitch!*" I shouted.

The driver jerked the wheel to the right, cutting me off and almost clipping my left front fender.

"Hang on, Kate," I said as I stamped on the brakes and moved even further to the right; I was quickly running out of road.

The Honda's brake lights flashed red. The car's speed dropped like a stone. I barely had a second to react. Gripping the wheel so hard my knuckles were white, I slammed on the brakes and the car screeched to a shuddering stop. The Honda also came to a stop some twenty yards farther on up the hard shoulder.

"What the hell is that guy's problem?" Kate shouted.

The Honda's driver's side door opened and out jumped Jeff Porter, an assault rifle in his hands and... he opened fire!

Chapter Thirty-Six

Friday Afternoon 5:45pm

A nanosecond later, Kate and I were in a firefight. Jeff had planted himself behind the Honda, some twenty yards away in front of my 2018 Range Rover, his rifle at his shoulder pointed straight at us. It had been a long time since I'd heard an automatic weapon at such close range. Even from twenty yards away, the sound was deafening.

I lifted my head as Jeff finished unloading his first magazine and felt a small sense of relief. Thankfully, I was one who took recent past experiences—and the paranoia they'd caused—into account. After my dealings with Shady Tree and his minions and in Mexico, I'd taken precautions. My Range Rover and Amanda's Jaguar F-Pace were/are built like tanks: reinforced windows and armored doors.

The windshield, totally spiderwebbed, was peppered with impacts from Porter's automatic weapon, but it was still pretty much intact. By the look of the impact points, I figured the weapon was firing 5.56 ammo: small but deadly.

Now I was really angry. My pride and joy was now riddled with bullet impacts, but I couldn't worry about that, not then. Jeffy boy was reloading.

The traffic everywhere had cleared the road. Porter was standing in the light of his headlights, trying to insert a fresh mag into his rifle.

We pulled our weapons, opened our doors and leaped out, using the doors for cover. Porter immediately began backing away and opened fire. The noise of his weapon and the bullets slamming into the armored doors was deafening, and even more so when we both returned fire.

Porter turned, ducked and ran around the front of the Honda. I heard him cry out in pain. One of us had clipped his thigh, but he was far from done. Crouching behind the Honda's hood, he continued shooting.

"This is insane!" Kate yelled, leaning out from behind her door to return fire a second time. "We can't keep this up. I'm running out of ammo."

"Stay locked on him," I yelled as my own weapon locked back, the mag empty. I'd fired fifteen rounds in less than a couple of minutes. I dropped the empty mag, inserted a full one—the only one I had left—released the slide and began to shoot.

And then, after another round of bullets from Porter's rifle, I heard something, a new sound, and boy was I glad to hear it: sirens.

They wailed in the distance. We were at the point where Riverfront Drive changes into Amnicola Highway, maybe twenty blocks from the police department, parked on the side of the road. *What a frickin' idiot, attacking us here.*

Clearly, Porter was still "the man from Arizona." And clearly, he had no idea where he was and less than sixty seconds away from being surrounded.

Porter must have heard the sirens, too, because he made his move.

He sprang out from behind his vehicle and took a shot at my head. I ducked. Kate returned fire, then I took aim as well. We just needed to wait for him to run out of rounds, or for the cavalry to arrive.

"I told you, Starke!" Porter yelled, taking a step closer. "But you didn't listen, did you? You stupid son of a—"

Bam!

Kate nailed him in his left shoulder. He faltered, looked stunned, staggered, then tried to bring his weapon to bear and fire again. I took the moment. I had a clear shot. I aimed and shot him in the gut. He got off one more round... I shot him in the neck.

He dropped his weapon, staggered backward, both hands at his neck, and then he fell to the ground. Kate and I cautiously stepped out from behind the doors and then ran toward him, our weapons pointed at him. He was gulping air, bleeding out on the road. He coughed, spraying blood from his mouth. Blood pumping out between his fingers. I figured he had but seconds left to live.

"This..." he began, his eyes wide, choking on his own blood, gasping and struggling to get his final words out. "This... was... supposed to be my redemption."

Then with a single gasp and a croak, his hands fell away from his neck, and he was gone.

To watch someone dying, especially after they'd been shot like that, is always unnerving.

Kate holstered her gun, crouched down beside him and checked his pulse, careful to avoid his wound.

"Well," she said as she got up again, "we got him..."

"This was supposed to be his redemption?" I asked.

"I don't know what that was supposed to mean," she said as five blue and whites screeched to a halt.

All of a sudden it was all flashing lights and the slamming of car doors as nine uniformed officers ran toward us, guns drawn.

Kate flashed her creds and the situation de-escalated. Most of them knew her anyway.

"It was supposed to be his redemption, and it became his execution," I said.

"Was he doing this on his own?" Kate asked. "Or... for someone else?"

I turned to her and said, with a grim smile on my lips, "Still think I'm being paranoid?"

Chapter Thirty-Seven

Friday Evening 6pm

It was at that point two ambulances and a fire truck arrived, along with Kate's best friend, once assistant chief, now captain, Henry Finkle; yes, I'm being facetious. She hates the man.

Me? I backed away into the shadows and called TJ.

"Hey, Harry. What's up man?"

I quickly explained what had happened. He was stunned, as I still was. That done, I said, "Listen, I need you to go to my house, right now. Please, I need you to make sure Amanda and Jade are safe and to make sure they stay that way."

"You got it, Harry," he said without a second thought. "I'm on my way." He hung up.

I exhaled deeply and stretched my neck. With TJ and Maria both at the house, I knew my family was in good hands. They were both armed and prepared to fight any and all intruders. Even so, I was antsy and wanted to go home.

Kate and I made our statements. We laid it out as far as

we knew it. We'd spoken to Porter earlier in the day. He'd threatened us and told us to back off. Then, he chased us down and tried to slaughter us. From his dying words, it seemed he was on a mission to redeem himself. Though what the hell that was supposed to mean, neither Kate nor I had any idea, though it did seem a little... weird, to say the least.

After we made our statements at the police department, there were a couple of police procedures we had to complete, one of which was the impounding of my car, covered as it was in impact craters.

I was practically sprinting through the processes. I knew them well, having been on the other side of the desk for more than eight years. Kate could tell I was itching to get out of there.

"I'll drive you home," she said.

I told her not to worry, that I had an Uber on the way and would have Amanda drive me to the rental shop early the next morning.

"What about your car?" she asked, a worried look on her face.

"Don't worry about it," I said. "I'll get it fixed. It's not in too bad of a shape. Most of the damage is cosmetic; the windshield? That's easily fixed. As soon as the PD releases it, I'll have it towed in."

She nodded and looked subdued.

"Are you okay?" I asked her.

"I'm all set, Harry. You do what you need to."

"Okay," I said. "You should go pick up Samson and go home and get some rest. We'll talk in the morning."

She nodded, and I thanked her and went to the front entrance to await my ride.

I glanced at the clock. It was six-fifty-five. We'd been

there for almost an hour. *Shit,* I thought, agitated that I wasn't already at home. I knew TJ was there, but still, the anxiety—maybe it *was* paranoia—was buzzing around inside my head. All bets were off. I wasn't just investigating the death of Benny Hinkle anymore. I'd become a target of the very people I'd been tracking down.

The Uber dropped me off on the road outside my house. I could see TJ's truck parked in the driveway, and I thanked God for it. I walked in through the open garage door, locked it down and marched into the house.

"Harry." TJ was standing in the entryway.

I gave him more details about the shootout with Jeff and repeated, verbatim, what he'd told me and Kate at the cafe.

"My car's a wreck, but the only one hit was Porter."

"God, Harry," TJ said. "You know I'm here for you whenever you need me, right?"

"I do, and I thank you for it, TJ," I said. "I can take it from here." Then I hugged him like a brother, had him wait for a minute while I grabbed a weapon since the police had confiscated mine, and sent him home.

Amanda was in the living room, on the couch, cradling Jade in her arms. Maria was standing at the window overlooking the driveway, a Glock 17 on the small, antique table beside her. I was beginning to feel a little better.

The house was secure and, of course, we had Maria. What does a nanny have to do with anything? You may well ask.

Maria Boylan is an enigma. When she came to me for a job as Jade's nanny, I was actually looking for a bodyguard for Amanda and Jade; Shady Tree was creating havoc in our lives. She's Hispanic, of average height, five-seven, and perhaps a little overweight, but not noticeably so. She was thirty-five then and had shoulder-length red hair—not her natural color—tied back in a ponytail, blue eyes and full lips. Her oval face was not unattractive, but there was a hardness about it that gave away her background. Even if I hadn't known, I would have pegged her as a cop.

She's a former ATF special agent— Alcohol, Tobacco, and Firearms—but she was dismissed... For what, I never found out, nor did I care. She was everything I was looking for, so I hired her on the spot and I haven't regretted it for a moment since.

"Harry!" Amanda cried out. She stood and hurried over to meet me, clutching Jade close to her chest.

"Hold on," I said. "I need to make sure everything is set."

I pushed past her and went straight to my office. All of the cameras were live. The motion detectors around the exteriors were all working, as were the door alarms. I also had firearms stashed at strategic locations around the house and even more in a gun safe in my office. We were prepared for just about everything.

"Harry, you're shaking," Amanda said as she followed me around the house, Jade still in her arms. "You're scaring me. Look at you, you're all worked up."

Dammit. I wasn't trying to worry her. I was just... being prepared.

"What happened, Harry?" she asked in a low voice.

"Amanda, I don't want to get into this; not right now."

That set her off.

"Harry, look at me!" she snapped. "What happened? Channel 7 has been pestering me. They told me there'd been a huge shootout on Amnicola, that *you* were caught up in it. Now, tell me what's going on or so help me God..."

She exhaled sharply through her nose and closed her eyes.

"Look," she said quietly, "I just want to know you're all right. Please, tell me you're okay. Tell me we're okay."

I couldn't lie to protect her. The car was now in impound, and the news at ten would tell her most of the story.

I leaned down and kissed Jade on the forehead, then gave Amanda a peck on the cheek. I held her shoulders and looked deep into her eyes.

"I'm okay. We're okay."

I led her back to the living room. Amanda handed Jade over to Maria, then we all sat down and I told them all what had happened... Well, not quite everything. I didn't need to tell them the gritty details of Porter's death.

"He was probably working alone," I continued. "But I want to be prepared just in case. Because if he was sent by some person or group, whoever it is, they're still out there."

I rested my face in my hands. Amanda scooted closer and wrapped her arms around me, resting her head on my shoulder.

She was right. I was shaking. You see, I knew Porter had been sent by someone, just as Diego Trejo had been sent to kill Franco, and all I could do was pray it wasn't another Shady Tree. That would have been a disaster in the making.

Maria put Jade down for the night and told us she'd sleep in her room on the daybed and not to worry. She'd keep an eye on her.

Amanda and I sat quietly together on the couch. Ten o'clock rolled around. It was time for the news. We skipped it that night. I had an idea I would be making the national news again, and that wasn't good.

"Feeling better?" she asked eventually.

I gave her a tired smile and nodded.

"Then let's get some sleep."

"You go," I said. "I'll sleep here on the couch."

"Oh, Harry."

"It's okay. I'm okay. I'll be fine."

She heaved a sigh, nodded and went to bed.

I wrapped myself in a blanket and tried to sleep. It must have been well after midnight when I finally drifted off, having reassured myself that we were safe.

For the moment.

Chapter Thirty-Eight

Saturday Morning 8:30am

K ate called bright and early the next morning, Saturday. She wanted to make sure Amanda and I were all right. She also wanted to give me a heads-up.

"Laura called me last night. She wanted to let me know they started redecorating at the Sorbonne. You want to go take a look?" Kate asked.

I thought about it for a minute, then said, "Ye...s, but you'll have to come pick me up. I don't have a car, remember?"

"No problem, sir. It's a lovely day for a ride up the mountain. How are you going to get back?"

I had to laugh at that. I knew she'd bring me back if I wanted her to, but I didn't. God only knew when I'd get my car back.

"I'll call the rental company," I said. "You can drop me off there."

Kate picked me up about forty-five minutes later. She

didn't come in. I told my family I'd be back by noon and I left them eating breakfast.

We parked out back on Prospect Street next to a newly delivered dumpster already half filled with debris and went inside.

Perhaps it was the chaos of the night before that made me so crabby. Kate seemed to have shrugged it off and was genuinely interested in Laura's and Trish's ideas; I couldn't pretend to feel the same. They thought a more metallic-looking wallpaper and some high-end neon signs behind the bar would brighten the place up. I didn't.

I joined Trish in the soon-to-be dining area. She had on her red cardigan again, and a small green bow in her hair. Snowflake earrings dangled from her ears.

"You've gotten a dose of Christmas spirit, I see," I said.

"My mom and I always loved this time of year," she replied. "We'd make these big batches of cinnamon rolls. She liked to make jewelry, too." She touched one of the snowflakes.

"She gave me these a couple of years back. I have reindeer and little ornament ones too, but these are my favorite with the little rhinestones."

She told me she brought them with her just in case. She hadn't been sure how long she'd be up here, but she wanted to be sure that if she stayed for the holiday, she'd have a piece of her mom with her.

Trish looked around the dining room, her eyes watering.

"There's an awful lot to do," she said.

"You're excited though, right?" I asked.

"Of course. It's fun, and Laura... she's nice."

"Well, then the work will be worth it," I said. "Your father left you this place and the money you need to remodel it. I think it's great."

And I actually did. "Most people come into money when they least expect it and make all kinds of mistakes, and it's soon gone. But you sure seem like you know what you're doing,"

Trish nodded, looked up at me and said, "Thanks, Harry. I know my dad thought a lot of you."

"And I thought a lot of him."

"Harry... I'm... scared."

I frowned. "Of what?"

"That you and the police are going to make me return all the money he left me. That it's not the kind of money anyone is supposed to have." She fidgeted with the bracelet on her wrist.

"I don't think that's likely to happen, Trish. There's no evidence that any of your father's money was illegally earned."

At least, not the inheritance, I thought.

She shifted away from the topic and started talking about the time they'd spent together in Atlanta. When he flew out to see her and she showed him around the city. She took out her phone. She'd set a photo of her and Benny as the background for her lock screen.

"This was the first one we took after we got in touch," she said. "I took him to an art gallery I really liked. I don't know how much fun it was for him, though." She smiled. "He didn't know what face to make for a selfie."

I chuckled. "That sounds like Benny."

She shook her head and pocketed her phone.

"He wasn't a good dad. I know that. I don't think he was even that good of a person. But he said he'd take care of me, and he has."

Her eyes wandered around the Sorbonne again.

My phone buzzed in my pocket, and I excused myself. It was Tim.

"Tim?" I asked. "You're supposed to be taking the weekend off."

"Harry," Tim said. "We've cracked it. Me and TJ. We really have. We just cracked it wide open."

"How? What did you find?"

"Okay, so, we found—"

Boom!

The front door slammed open. Someone had kicked it in, and a half-dozen men rushed in, all wearing camo, black hoods that covered their faces, and all armed with assault rifles.

"Everyone, on the ground, now!" one of them yelled.

Kate and Laura, who were standing by the bar, got down on their knees, their hands up. Trish gasped, and then she and I did the same.

I locked eyes with Kate. She shook her head. She was right. There was no point in pulling our weapons. That would have been an invitation for any or all of them to open fire. Even Moose, who was posted inside the front door, was down on his knees.

"Who are you?" I asked. "What do you want?"

One of them, the one that had yelled at us to get down, walked over to me, the end of the barrel of his weapon pointed at me.

We locked eyes. His narrowed. It looked as if he was grinning at me.

"We want you, Mr. Starke," he said lightly. "You're to come with us."

Oh goody. They're here to see me.

I pushed the sarcastic thought out of my head and rose to my feet, my hands up. What was happening was beginning to sink in and I was, not exactly terrified, but I wasn't too happy about it either.

The leader and three men surrounded me and walked me back to Benny's office. I heard another thug back in the bar warning everyone not to get smart.

"If any of you move, we're going to decorate the walls with the back of your head."

I was shoved into Benny's office and told to turn around and keep my hands over my head. I found myself facing the four of them.

All four of them, in synchrony, cocked their weapons, shouldered them and pointed them at me.

I'm here to tell you that at that moment, my whole body went numb.

So, I thought. *This is how it ends?*

Chapter Thirty-Nine

Saturday Morning 10am

But it wasn't. Two more armed men stepped inside and joined the party. I could see through the open door that there were even more standing out in the hallway.

What the hell? I thought. *Who are these people, and what do they want with me?*

"Sit down," the leader said.

And I did. Carefully! My hands still in the air.

One of the men who'd just joined stepped over to Benny's desk, rolled his chair around and set it in front of me. Then, he cleaned it, wiping the seat with what appeared to be a handkerchief from his pocket. But he didn't sit down.

What the hell?

"Your gun and cell phone, please, Mr. Starke."

Carefully, I handed them over and he placed them on the desk. Then two of the men took two steps back and stood behind me, one to my left, the other to my right.

And then there was a moment of silence. The other four just stood there looking at me, saying nothing. Then, the group parted in the center and they lowered their weapons slightly.

"Ma'am!" one of them shouted.

Ma'am?

And there she was. The white-haired woman from the poker games.

She was dressed in a black business suit; the skirt cut just below the knees. In person, she didn't look as old as she had in the videos. I figured she was around fifty, give or take a couple of years, slim, nice figure. There were the beginnings of crow's feet around her eyes and permanent frown lines across her forehead. Her eyes were blue. Her skin had a subtle shine to it. Regardless of her age and makeup, she was... beautiful. Her presence and demeanor reminded me of a lady senator from Boston I once knew.

She sat down, crossed her legs, clasped her hands together in her lap and looked at me.

"Harry Starke," she said. "We meet at last." Her voice was soft, her enunciation clear.

"Who are you?" I asked. "You know my name. What's yours?"

"I didn't come here to get to know you, Harry." The look she gave me was one that would have struck fear in anyone. Her eyes narrowed. The frown lines deepened, and her lips tightened. This was a powerful woman.

"You've been meddling in things that don't concern you," she said.

"I don't see how," I replied. "I'm working a murder case. How does that concern you?"

She coyly rested her tongue on her teeth for a moment,

the edges of her mouth spreading into a smile. She glossed over that question with a simple shake of her head.

"The reason I'm here is to make a simple request," she said. "One I'm sure you'll appreciate."

"I'm listening."

"I'm asking you nicely to cease your investigation. Right here. Right now."

"And if I don't?"

"That would be very stupid of you, Harry, and you're not a stupid man, are you?"

I didn't know how to answer that one, so I just shook my head.

"Good. You wouldn't want anything to happen to that lovely wife and daughter of yours, now would you?"

"No!" I snapped.

Her posture was impeccable, and she somehow made even the threat sound alluring. I was dealing with a cold-hearted killer, and I knew without a doubt that she meant every word she said.

"So we have a deal then?" she asked. "You'll close your investigation?"

"I will, but the police won't."

"You let me worry about that. Do we have a deal or not?" she snapped.

I set my jaw and nodded, not taking my eyes off hers.

"We do. I get the message."

That coy smile returned and her face softened.

Then, she looked around the circle of men and nodded.

Something hit me in the back of the head and everything went black.

Chapter Forty

Saturday Morning 10:45am

"Harry! Harry! Can you hear me?"

It was as if I was coming out of a cold dark cave into the light to find Laura at my side on her knees bent over me. Her cold hands gently tapped my cheeks. I blinked several times, trying to focus.

"Hey," I muttered finally. "How... long? How long was I out?"

"They left just a couple of minutes ago, all of them." She'd been crying. I sat up and rubbed the back of my head. There was a lump the size of an egg and I had a splitting headache.

She sat leaning back on her knees. "I thought we were all going to die. Who *were* they?" Her voice sounded dry.

"I don't know. They didn't introduce themselves," I quipped. "Where's Kate?"

"She's talking to the police."

I asked her if anyone else was hurt. Fortunately, no one was.

I struggled to my feet, gave Laura a hand up, then grabbed my gun and phone from Benny's desk. Then I stood for a moment, trying to get my balance.

Where the hell did all those soldiers come from? I wondered. *And how in God's name were they able to simply walk out of here and disappear; in downtown Chattanooga?*

It didn't take the cops and an ambulance long to arrive. They checked us all out. I didn't need medical attention. I'd had worse bumps on my head. All I needed was a couple of aspirin. What I needed to do was to get to my office and talk to Tim and TJ and try to figure out what the hell had just happened.

We left the bar in a state of chaos. Laura was crying like a baby and Trish was trying to comfort her. I would have liked to have stayed, but I didn't have time.

Kate was in one hell of a rush. The chief had called while I was with Laura in the office. He wanted to see her. She had some explaining to do. The rental company was less than five minutes away, so she dropped me there and then sped off to the PD.

It was almost mid-day when I arrived at my office, my head aching like... It was aching, okay?

I walked into the lobby and everyone jumped on me wanting to know if I was all right and asking questions. Kate had called Jacque, and she'd come into the office right away.

"Are you sure you're okay?" Jacque asked.

"Yeah, I'm fine, but I need coffee. D'you think—"

"Go to your office and sit down," Jacque replied. "I'll get it." The Jamaican accent was on full display and I couldn't help but smile.

I turned to TJ and Tim. "What did you find? That thing you were going to tell me earlier on the phone."

"Well..." Tim began. "You sure you're okay, boss?"

"Just get on with it, Tim," I said as I dropped into my seat behind my desk.

He nodded, then continued, "Some of it you already know. That woman is the one calling the shots. I kept watching the footage, and finally I figured out what was going on. I think Jeff Porter was working for her. Over the course of a game, she had this signal thing where she'd play with her earring. Porter would then bet on her losing hand. Then the money would go to one or the other. I don't know how we missed it. I don't think even Benny saw it."

"I'm not surprised Benny didn't catch it," TJ said softly. "But, this little trick Jeff and the woman pulled happened at every game."

Me, I was surprised. Four of the players—all crooks—and Benny had been playing with this woman, and they had no idea who she was. Hell, I didn't know who she was. I asked them if they'd found out anything else about her or about Porter, who was obviously on her payroll.

"Well, I did find a little tidbit," Tim said. "Ravern Solutions where Porter said he worked... It doesn't exist."

"I have something for you too," TJ said and began tapping on his iPad.

My phone rang. It was Kate.

"Harry, we can't find those people anywhere. Not even on CCTV. I don't know how because they had a whole squad of vans driving away from here."

She sounded out of breath.

"Harry, I need to know what happened in that office? What'd they say? Who knocked you out?"

I wasn't really listening to her. The wheels were spinning in my head. The crew that attacked us was too sophisticated to have murdered Benny like that. They wouldn't have left the cameras behind. Hell, they wouldn't have even left the body behind. But, if it wasn't the woman and her crew, who the hell was it?

I told Kate I needed a minute and I put her on hold; not a smart thing to do, ever.

I put my phone on the desk and looked at TJ.

"What have you got?" I asked.

He handed me his iPad. There was a document on the screen. It was a purchase order for micro video recording equipment.

The buyer? *No shit? Are you frickin' kidding me?*

"You were right, Harry," TJ said. "He was getting involved."

I picked up my phone. Kate was still holding, and she was irate.

"Harry? Don't you ever do that to me again. Do you hear me?"

"Kate... Kate. Shut the hell up and come and get me. I know who killed Benny Hinkle!"

Chapter Forty-One

Saturday Morning Noon

While I was waiting for Kate, I called Perks' office. *Waste of time,* I thought. *It's Saturday.*

"I don't suppose Mr. Perks is in today?" I asked hopefully.

"No sir, I'm sorry. He's at home. He's not feeling well today."

I thanked her and hung up. At least we knew where he was.

Tim gave me his address just as Kate flipped her siren on and off outside. I rushed outside and leaped into her car. I punched the location into my phone and told her to drive.

"For the final time," she said as she pulled out of the parking lot, "what happened at the Sorbonne?"

I'd been dreaming up a fake story in my head while I was waiting for her.

"They sat me down in the office and wanted to know what happened to Jeff Porter," I lied. "They wanted to know how he died and if he'd had any last words. I told them the truth, and they knocked me out and left... Kate, I think they were spooks, CIA, NSA or something even more... black." Why I told her that last, I don't know. The words just seem to spill out.

"Yeah, that's what I figured too," she said. To my surprise, hers was a similar story.

"Only, they didn't ask us any questions. They just had us put our phones and my weapon on the bar. Then, we had to stay on the ground until your little meeting was done..."

"And after that, they left," I finished for her.

"So, you think Perks is our killer?" she said, changing the subject, much to my relief. I didn't want to mention the woman and her threat, not then anyway. We had a killer to catch.

"Oh yes. He bought the video equipment: the micro cameras, microphones and knew where the cameras were. He must have had someone else install them. Who, I don't know; someone he hired to do the job, I guess."

"But why? What the hell was going on, Harry?"

"I don't know, not for sure. Maybe when we talk to him, we'll find out."

"So, he killed Benny," Kate said.

"Yes. And now he's sick. Getting sicker and sicker."

"How do you know that?"

"He's got a real nasty infection. Gunshot wound." I smiled at her.

"He messed up coming to my office, Kate," I continued. "He demanded an update on the investigation. I knew in my gut something was amiss. He outsmarted himself. He didn't need to know, but he couldn't help himself. I think he was hoping we'd hang the murder on Franco or someone at the poker game. And he made sure we'd know who they were. He left that camera behind so we'd get a good look at the players."

We arrived at Perks' house at a little after twelve noon. It was, as you'd expect, a nice home in an exclusive neighborhood. His car was in the driveway.

"How d'you want to do this?" Kate asked.

I grinned at her. "Through the front door, of course."

We mounted the three steps onto the front porch. Kate drew her weapon and gave me a nod.

I kicked in the door, drew my own weapon and followed her inside. We stood for a moment listening.

I heard someone cuss in a hoarse voice.

We advanced through the foyer into a huge, sparsely furnished, open-plan area. We stepped down into the living room area, and there, lying on his couch, was Bill Perks. He looked terrible. His skin had a yellow hue. His body was drenched in sweat. And his expression was one of a sour pig.

"Get the hell out of my house," he spat. He could barely lift himself up on the couch.

"Not very menacing, Bill," I said. "Lift up your shirt."

He didn't say anything, his eyes going from me to Kate, then back to me. Then, he grunted, and with shaking hands, he pulled up his T-shirt.

"There you go," I said as I looked down at the ulcerous gunshot wound. "That's why you need to treat a gunshot wound. So that it doesn't go septic."

The wound was right in his side. He'd done his best to cover it with gauze. There was significant bruising around the area, and it appeared to me that the bandage was stuck to his body. It was soaked with blood and yellow puss. I told Kate to call an ambulance.

"It was you that night at the Sorbonne, wasn't it?" I asked.

He lay there, flat out, utterly defeated.

"Yes. And you shot me, you son of a bitch."

"Oh come now, Bill. You shot at me first. What was I supposed to do?"

He didn't answer.

"What were you looking for?" I asked.

Again he said nothing.

"It was the equipment you had installed, wasn't it?" I took a step toward him. He wasn't armed.

"That greedy bastard pulled the mics." Perks yelped as he tried to sit up.

He somehow made it into a sitting position and leaned on his knees. His eyes were watery, with a dark, purple hue around them.

"I didn't know he did it until he told me. That audio was supposed to be my insurance."

"So you killed him."

Bill threw his head back in resignation. He leaned back into his couch.

"I thought the fat bastard was too dumb to figure it out. Too stupid to find the mics. But he found one and pulled it. Then the other. Said he needed his own insurance."

"You helped him orchestrate everything. Set it all up? Sent him the poker players?"

"Yes, he was buying and selling seedy secrets. You have no idea the stuff he had on some serious people in this town. He was making a killing."

"So he was blackmailing them?" Kate asked.

"N...ah," he creaked. "He was just selling it back to them... He found out I was... taking money from my client's accounts, and he was threatening to sell the information to them."

"So he was blackmailing you?" Kate asked.

"Nah. He was just being an asshole. He didn't want money from me. Anything I could have paid him he'd gotten ten times over from my clients, and I would have gone to jail. So, yes. I was just so frickin' mad that I killed the fat little bastard."

Kate looked at me and said, "The ambulance is on its way." She took out her handcuffs, shook her head and put them back again.

"William Perks, you're under arrest for the murder of Benny Hinkle."

"The name's not William," he muttered. "It's Bill. It's on my birth certificate."

Chapter Forty-Two

Tuesday Evening 7pm

Christmas Eve finally arrived and I'd given everyone the day off. We'd all agreed to meet at the Sorbonne around seven for a drink, a little private get-together.

Amanda and I had spent a lazy day around the house, playing with Jade and listening to holiday music, just enjoying each other's company. Her present arrived that morning.

By six o'clock we were ready to leave. "We'll be back by ten, Maria," Amanda told her before she and I went to get ready.

It was to be a casual affair so we both wore jeans. Amanda wore a white top with hers. I wore a white and blue striped dress shirt

"I have something for you to wear tonight," I said.

She smiled and raised her eyebrows. "What?"

I told her to turn around. I took the necklace from my

pocket and fastened the thin gold chain around her neck and turned her around.

"Happy Christmas, sweetheart."

She put her hand to it and rushed to the mirror. I followed her.

It was a simple little thing, a gold pendant with an eighteen-karat pear cut emerald. She's always loved green.

"I didn't know if I should wrap it..." I'd prepared what I wanted to say and now I was falling over my tongue.

"I'm so grateful that you're here, in my life," I said, finding the words. "You and Jade. You've both been through too much because of me. I want everything to be better and—"

Amanda took my hand and smiled, put her fingers to my lips and said, "Thank you. It's... simply beautiful."

"Emeralds are supposed to be for new beginnings," I said. "I want you, and Jade, to have something to look forward to. Something to hold on to."

She smiled up at me, stood on tiptoe, kissed me and then said, "As long as you're by our side, that's all we need."

* * *

"Yay, now the gang's all here," Laura cheered as we walked into the Sorbonne that evening. And, she was right. Jacque, Heather, Tim, TJ and all the rest of my team were there, all smiles. Each of them was holding a mug with a cinnamon stick and sprig of rosemary poking out the top.

Even Kate and Samson had made it.

I gave Amanda's arm a squeeze, told her I'd be just a minute, then stepped away to speak to her.

"Merry Christmas, Kate."

"Right back at ya, partner."

I was stunned. She hadn't called me that in more than ten years.

She nodded in Amanda's direction and said, "Does she like it? Wow, it's even nicer in person. If she doesn't, you can pass it my way."

I laughed. "She does. Thank you, Kate. Come and say hello." And she did.

Trish was behind the bar with Laura, serving drinks.

"Laura showed me how to make Christmas mules," she said. "I didn't realize there'd be this steep of a learning curve!"

When everyone had their drinks, Laura called a toast.

"Attention, everyone. I'd like you all to raise your glasses and drink a toast. 'To Benny, may you rest in peace, my friend.'"

"To Benny," we all responded.

By the time we were finished that evening, we'd all decided that he was actually a pretty good guy.

While I was relieved that the case was closed, when Laura mentioned that we'd caught his killer I glanced around at the rest of my crew. We had indeed caught the killer, but their stiff smiles told me that none of us were satisfied.

True, the poker players had nothing to do with Benny's death, but they were all guilty of illegal activities of one sort or another. I had the idea I wasn't yet finished with Franco de Luca. And then there was the puppet master; the white-haired, mysterious woman.

It was about an hour later when I decided I needed some air and stepped out onto the street. It was a beautiful night. The sky was clear and full of stars, and there was a slight breeze blowing in off the river. I savored the moment, standing there alone with my thoughts.

What the hell is her game? I wondered. *And why me? Why did she threaten me? Who the hell is she? So many questions and not a single answer.*

The more I thought about it, the more puzzled I became. One thing I was sure of, though, was that woman was still out there and, one way or another, I'd be meeting her again... soon.

"Hey, you. A penny for them?" Kate said, breaking into my thoughts.

I turned around. She was standing in the open doorway.

I nodded. "I just... needed some air, cool off a bit, you know?"

She nodded.

"You okay?" I asked.

She nodded, stepped out of the doorway and joined me. She wrapped her scarf more tightly around her neck and put her hands in her pockets.

"Harry, what the hell happened the other night?"

"What d'you mean?"

"You know what I mean." She smirked. "What did that woman want with you?"

"How did you know about her?" I asked.

"I saw her, dumb ass."

"She told me to back off, is all," I replied.

"And you agreed, right?"

"What do you think?" I asked.

Well, at least I didn't lie to her, did I?

The End

Made in the USA
Coppell, TX
27 October 2022